"You said on the phone that you're into wild things."

The comment made him smile. It was a wolfish kind of smile that he wouldn't normally wear. "You're into the same things, right?"

He knew Tamara was playing a game of verbal foreplay.

"Wild as in…?"

Murphy slipped his fingers into her high collar to smooth over her nape. He heard her intake of breath.

"As in—" he whisked his fingertips down to the small of her back, where he started drawing slow circles "—anything goes."

"I don't really even know you from Adam," she said.

She'd said the right words, revving him up with the reminder that he'd left himself behind. He was devil-may-care Kyle, not Murphy, the guy who always did what was expected of him.

"Then we need to do something about getting acquainted," he whispered.

He knew she could leave right now. But she wasn't moving. Maybe this woman in thigh-high boots could give Murphy what he needed.

A taste of bad.

Blaze™

Dear Reader,

Welcome to the Wentworth-Holt Building, where a bunch of intelligent and lively women have banded together to beat the single-girl blues in a novel way!

When Alison Kent first approached me about writing a miniseries with her, I didn't hesitate. Then when Nancy Warren came on board it was a dream come true. What we ended up with was this plan for some women to take back control of their social lives: a lottery-type system involving a funky glass vase, business cards and plenty of steamy encounters.

I hope you have a lot of fun with FOR A GOOD TIME CALL… during the next few months. In this series finding a playmate is the name of the game….

Enjoy,

Crystal Green
www.crystal-green.com

INNUENDO
Crystal Green

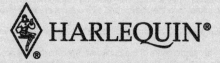

TORONTO • NEW YORK • LONDON
AMSTERDAM • PARIS • SYDNEY • HAMBURG
STOCKHOLM • ATHENS • TOKYO • MILAN • MADRID
PRAGUE • WARSAW • BUDAPEST • AUCKLAND

ISBN-13: 978-0-373-79265-8
ISBN-10: 0-373-79265-4

INNUENDO

ABOUT THE AUTHOR

Crystal Green lives near Las Vegas, Nevada, where she writes Harlequin Blaze, Silhouette Special Edition and Silhouette Bombshell novels, plus Berkley vampire tales. She loves to read, overanalyze movies, do yoga and write about her obsessions on her Web page, www.crystal-green.com. Like Tam Clarkson, the heroine of *Innuendo*, Crystal loves to travel, and you can see photo-treks about her trips to Japan and Italy on the site, too.

Books by Crystal Green

HARLEQUIN BLAZE

SILHOUETTE SPECIAL EDITION

Don't miss any of our special offers. Write to us at the following address for information on our newest releases.

Harlequin Reader Service
U.S.: 3010 Walden Ave., P.O. Box 1325, Buffalo, NY 14269
Canadian: P.O. Box 609, Fort Erie, Ont. L2A 5X3

To Joan, my sister-in-law, for providing a bit
of her single life as story fodder,
and to Mica and Nancy, partners in creativity.
Here's to the creation of the Sisters of the Booty Call!

1

"YOU, MS. TAMARA CLARKSON, need some booty."

At the cheeky words, Tam laughed and turned away from her computer keyboard. Normally she used it to enter information into the Dillard Marketing database as part of her temporary gig. But right now there were no assignments on her desk, so she'd been covertly scribbling down a new personal budget that she would never complete anyway, what with her being the mistress of be-ginning-many-projects-but-hardly-ever-finishing-them.

The speaker, Danica Langston, was wiggling her eyebrows in mischief while leaning against Tam's cubicle. The mild sunshine of a San Francisco September afternoon breathed through the windows and dusted her coworker's dark skin.

This was Tam's first temp job in her new home city. Since being assigned to Dillard two weeks ago, she and Danica had become friends, mainly by bonding through the curse of being single women in the city. Over lunch, they would complain about men and then look out the window to people-watch the nine-to-fivers strolling along the sidewalks of the Financial District. It was a daily rit-ual—except for Mondays. Danica never failed to disap-pear that day, always claiming an "essential meeting."

So Danica's next words came as a surprise. "Ready for a lunch break?"

Tam raised an eyebrow. "No meeting today?"

"Sure, but you're coming with me this time." Danica motioned for Tam to get out of her chair. "I've got some friends I want you to meet. Then we'll grab some quick grub afterward and bring it back up here."

From booty to networking. What a segue. Intrigued, Tam closed her computer program and gathered her purse. She hadn't met many people in the city yet, so this was a good opportunity. Aside from the anything-but-shy Danica, the Dillard dungeon didn't seem to hire many outgoing individuals.

Yup, it was tough to make friends here. Bummer, since all Tam wanted to do since she'd moved to San Fran from her family home in Vegas was to start fresh. Here, in a city teeming with good vibes, she could finally ditch all the temp work and find the job she was meant for. Then she could earn enough money for a place of her very own—one she could decorate and celebrate her freedom in. And Tam was optimistic that she would accomplish at least the job part by next summer.

Freedom, she thought. San Francisco, with its hippy history and open-air poetry, was just the place to discover it.

Liar, said a little voice inside. *You want security. You can tell yourself you'd love to be free all you want, but it isn't the answer. You try to crave it because you think it means you don't need anyone, and that way you'll never feel rejection again.*

Freedom is just a lie for you....

Tam knew that voice. It was the whisper of a hurt

child who'd been shoved deep down where she could never be wounded again by reminders of her parents' divorce. She folded the voice to the back of her mind where it couldn't be heard anymore, and instead donned a perky smile for Danica. It worked every time to fool the world—to fool herself, too.

"So…meetings," she said as they left the office. "Are you in some kind of social club?"

"You could say that."

They caught the elevator, finding themselves alone. With a mysterious grin, Danica pressed the second-floor button, then leaned toward the shiny brass panel and primped, running her manicured hands over the short, dark pageboy cut she wore.

But Tam didn't look in the makeshift mirror. She knew exactly what she would see: a longer-than-average face framed by shoulder-length, thick, curly hair, light brown bordering on mousy. She would also find lips that were usually spread into a smile, and a pair of aquamarine eyes: the kind of color that, normally, you could only cheat into existence with contacts.

The shape of her face—and her long nose—had bothered her ever since a pivotal moment in middle school when Jimmy Denning had poked fun at them, calling her "horse face," causing an entire lunch table full of kids to laugh at her. Since her parents' divorce had made her sensitive to rejection, she'd taken it hard and to heart. But she *hadn't* taken it lying down; no, from that point on, she'd tried to distract everyone from noticing her face with a flamboyant wardrobe and a sunny personality, and it had worked. If everyone concentrated on her surface, they wouldn't bother with what lay beneath, she reasoned.

It was her safety net—one she fantasized about leaving behind. And if San Francisco could change her into a free spirit with no worries, then maybe she'd finally be able to just be herself.

At least, she hoped so.

Tam plucked at her intricate, bold, Haight-Ashbury vintage skirt, getting anxious about this meeting of Danica's. With any luck, everyone's attention would be drawn to her clothes, not her face. But if they did focus in on her mug? Yup, she'd be smiling.

And hoping they wouldn't look past that.

She turned to her friend. "I guess maybe all those comments I made at lunch about meeting men in a new town painted me as a desperate nympho or something?"

Danica laughed. "No more than the rest of us."

The rest of…who, exactly?

The elevator arrived at floor two, where the scent of herbs and perfumed lotions welcomed them. They stepped off, headed to a day spa called Indulge, then into a restroom at the end of the hall.

"A bathroom?" Not exactly The Ritz.

"Privacy and proximity for our secret meetings." Smiling, Danica placed her hand against the door. "Now, you don't need to take part in anything today, all right?"

"You're killin' me. What's going on?"

The other woman bit her lower lip, showing dimples. Then she said cryptically, "Just the single-girl blues, baby, the single-girl blues."

Tam started to ask for more of an answer, but her friend had already opened the door.

Single-girl blues. Tam sure had a catalog of those.

By choice, she hadn't dated in about a year. Even at twenty-five, she was bone weary of failure, of going on two dates with a guy then having him lose interest. She didn't have the energy to try again right now. Besides, her new start here in San Fran didn't include getting a boyfriend. Yet. If ever.

But…okay, yeah. Tam would admit that, truthfully, she was lonely. That trying just one more time, if she could talk herself into it, might mean finally tripping over a decent guy. Yet "one more time" never seemed to happen.

As they entered, Tam saw that there was a tiny waiting area that opened into two directions: toilets to the right and a lounge to the left. There, among the flower-scented dignity of potted plants, silk flowers, burgundy carpet, chintz upholstery and a gilded mirror, waited a group of women. Dressed in business clothes, they sat on the couch and matching chairs, leafing through the estrogen-inspired magazines on the mahogany coffee table, chatting and laughing.

On the middle of the table stood a glass vase, its etched designs catching the soft light, making it glimmer. Shaped like a cowboy boot, it held, not flowers, but a bevy of small white papers.

Business cards?

"Hey!" Danica said to the group.

Everyone jovially said hello, not seeming to mind that Tam was in their midst. A sultry woman with black hair and equally dark eyes, her long body draped like silk over the couch, welcomed the new arrivals in a voice that was polished with the hint of an exotic accent. Tam knew her name: Mercedes Estevez, the owner of Indulge.

Self-conscious in the face of this woman's beauty, Tam went back to fidgeting with her skirt, expertly drawing Mercedes's attention away from her crazy hair, her homely face. Today she sported a shimmering silk blouse rolled to the elbows; it complemented her skirt and was accentuated by a long, delicate silver chain that draped over her hips like webbing. Earrings that dangled like rainfall, plus matching pumps that had chains as straps, rounded out her artful fashion arrangement.

"Everyone," Danica said, "this is who I told you about last week. Tamara Clarkson."

"Welcome to our Sisters of the Booty Call meeting," said a woman with leopard-skin pumps and spiked brown hair.

When she motioned toward the glass boot vase, everyone laughed. Tam guessed it was because of her "Oh, that's what Danica meant by booty?" look. She pumped up her smile wattage.

Another woman shook Tam's hand, her green eyes friendly. She wore her blond hair in short, chin-length layers—a model of urban hip. "I'm Milla Page. Tenth floor, from that tiny office of Web geeks."

"MatchMeUpOnline.com is one of your sites," Tam said, shaking Milla's hand in return. She was a fan of the site, with its club, restaurant and hot spot suggestions. Perfect for singles planning a night out.

As the other women greeted her and introduced themselves, Tam settled into a seat, meeting Danica's gaze. Her coworker's eyes were hopeful, as if she was holding her breath that Tam would fit into the crowd.

Heck, Tam was wondering how it would go, too. But…so far so good, right?

As other women entered and made themselves comfortable, they all small-talked, drawing a few personal details out of Tam. She'd graduated from UNLV over three years ago. She'd become a perpetual temporary worker until she could find the job of all jobs because she wasn't about to settle for anything less, like the one she had at Dillard Marketing. Her most recent noteworthy relationship had been one year ago, lasting an amazing two months....

When the women seemed surprised at Tam's lack of a love life, she quickly added that she was a commitmentphobe. True, it was a simplified explanation for her much deeper issues, but they bought it.

In the middle of it all, The Boot waited, gleaming under the light.

A woman who'd introduced herself as Julia Nguyen caught Tam's curious glance.

"Shall we?" she asked the others, gesturing toward the vase and then Tam. She was slender and sat upright in her chair, her speech flavored with the cadence of Little Saigon.

"I think she's perfect for us," said the woman with leopard-print pumps.

Before Tam could even smile in response, Danica bounded to her side, taking a seat on the arm of the couch. "Great!" Glowing, she turned to Tam. "Just promise one thing—that you won't breathe a word about our Monday meetings outside this lounge. That's a requirement."

Bursting at the seams for answers, Tam nodded.

"We don't bring our office work in here, and we don't bring what goes on in here to the office," said Julia Nguyen, clearly the group taskmaster.

"Got it." Tam glanced around the room. "So why's there a glass boot on the table, and why is it full of business cards?"

A regally husky voice behind Tam spoke up. "I'll just make this long story short, if you girls don't mind."

Tam's attention swiveled to a woman with platinum ringlets who leaned against the wall, one long leg crossed over the other, arms loosely folded over her chest. She'd already introduced herself as Pamela Hoff. Statuesque and lean, she was the queen of the lounge.

When she caught Tam's eye, she grinned, eyebrows arching devilishly as she leaned forward. Without even a word, it was obvious that this was a tale the lady loved to tell.

"This all officially started when I went out with a man who was some kind of urban cowboy—I mean, imagine a guy from Detroit dressed in a bolo and a Shady Brady who uses a Roy Rogers lighter and talks like John Wayne. A real charmer who kept spitting tobacco into his champagne glass like it was no huge breach of social etiquette. And that's when it hit me." She held up her hands in a motion of epiphany. "I couldn't take the disappointments anymore. So I told the guy that I wasn't going to be around for a second date, then went home and made serious plans to go celibate."

Tam could pretty much relate to that.

The woman with the leopard-print pumps snorted in patent disbelief. Teena. Yeah, that was her name. Fifteenth floor financial consultant. She'd already spelled "T-e-e-n-a" for Tam in her Southern-fried accent.

"Really, Teena, I was *this* close." Pamela measured a tiny space between her thumb and forefinger. "Then the guy started calling me, as if our date had gone really well and he couldn't catch a clue even if it was running straight at him. That was the final straw. I knew I wouldn't last another second dating in this city if this was how it was going to go every time. I felt like I had no control anymore. So I took it back. When he sent me flowers and asked me out yet again, I responded in the only way he'd understand."

In her lush accent, Mercedes Estevez pointed to the glass vase and said, "When he showed up at the office to see if she'd gotten the flowers..."

Everyone but Tam joined in, like it was a communal punchline. "She gave *him* the boot."

They all laughed together.

"He just wasn't getting the hint over the phone," Pamela continued, so energized by her story that she'd pushed away from the wall, eyes sparkling and voice raised. "So I tucked his posies into the waistband of his Wrangler jeans and followed them up with this vase full of water to cool off—" her hands searched for words in the air.

"—his little cowpoke?" Teena provided.

Tam couldn't help laughing along with everyone. A fun crowd, she thought, thinking it was good to be a part of one. For the first time, she had an inkling of what it would be like to be among her own kind.

"From that point on," Danica added, "Pamela created a sort of dating service." She pulled a card out of her blouse pocket. "Every week, we meet here to pool resources. You know how you go to a bar or a social event and you hit it off with a guy? He usually gives you his business card. Well, we're putting them to good use now. If I meet a man and I know that he isn't quite my cup of java but he still seems like a good catch, I accept his card, then write a note on the back—'Great sense of humor, but I am morally opposed to men wearing Bugs Bunny ties.' That sort of thing. Then I come to work on Monday—" Danica deposited her card in the vase "—put the card I acquired in The Boot, then draw a different one for me. If I like the description of the man, I call the number and yadadee, yadadoo."

A long-haired brunette with a name Tam couldn't recall picked up the vase and started to mix the cards lottery-style while Teena jumped in.

"We've pretty much screened the men for each other. It's not a perfect system—sometimes a creep or two slimes through the cracks—but they always make for a good Monday story."

Pamela's voice rang out again. "And the beauty of it is that you don't need to go into it thinking you'll end up with this man forever." She went back to her stance against the wall, folding her arms across her chest again. "I sure as hell don't."

Tam didn't really know what to say or if this was even something she should consider taking part in. It was exciting to have a vaseful of opportunity within reach… but daunting. It'd been so long since she'd been out in the dating world. Did she even *have* social skills anymore?

God, she wasn't sure. It was nice that they'd decided she was the perfect candidate, but none of them had any idea just how exhausted Tam was, just how many guys she'd tried to connect with and failed. To complicate matters, the failures were likely caused by her sabotaging the relationships before the men could abandon *her*.

She thought about the last pseudo-affair: John Yarborough. They'd go out for a movie and dinner, get it on, then take up where they'd left off the next weekend. The thing was, their interaction had never gone anywhere beyond the sex-and-cinema nights.

What was it about her that made people—men, her own mother—want to leave?

No matter, she thought. She'd done everything she could to protect herself from ever hurting again: taking jobs as a temp, dating a chain of guys who, in retrospect, showed no inkling of constancy….

Yet something Pamela had said stuck with Tam.

The beauty of it is that you don't need to go into it thinking you'll end up with this man forever.

They made it sound so easy, as if *she* had control over what could happen.

"Listen," Danica said, sympathy in her gaze. "If you don't want to do it, don't. But I know you're ready for this. It's just a way to find a good time and get to know more people. Who knows? You could meet your best guy friend out there. And you can trust the recommendation of every woman here. We're like you—decent, hardworking…a little horny."

Echoes of amused agreement sounded throughout the room, accompanied by a couple of encouraging looks directed at Tam.

The Boot was placed back on the table.

"Why don't you sit back and watch how it works?" Teena said. "Then you can decide if it's what you want."

While Tam listened as the women began their ritual by sharing their dating adventures from over the weekend, she wished she could tell them that she would give anything if they could guarantee a man who treated her as naturally and nicely as they had. A man who would allow her to finally be that footloose-and-fancy-free woman who was in charge of her own destiny and feelings, a woman who did more than just dress the part. He didn't have to be her soul mate—jeez, she'd prefer that he wasn't at this point, because she wasn't ready to settle down—just a playmate would be nice.

Yeah, she thought, warming up to the idea. A light, casual thing. A baby step. She still didn't have the energy to try for anything more yet. Not until she'd accomplished her goal of finding *herself*.

As the conversation continued, the women's stories ranged from sad to optimistic to funny. A few women, including Julia Nguyen, had even planned for second dates this weekend with the same guys.

All too soon, it was time to draw from the vase. Tam held her breath as Danica went first.

Her coworker held the card up to her face; she'd left her reading glasses in the office. Squinting, she said, "Dana Didrickson, attorney at law."

"Oooo," Teena said. "That was mine!"

Danica lowered the card. "He's got a girl's name."

"Read my comment, would you?"

Squinting again, Danica continued. "'Polite, smart, witty, but might need a woman who is up to the challenge of dragging him away from the office.'"

Teena was shaking her finger in the air. "He's a good one, but I've had my fill of workaholics."

Tam glanced at her lap. She understood Teena all too well. Her own dad had lapsed into the office disease after divorcing her mom. True, he'd still showered Tam with affection, usually in the form of money, and he'd petitioned for custody—and won—but that didn't mean life without him at the dinner table every night was easy.

Danica had popped to her feet, a bundle of energy. "I'm up for a challenge, baby. Bring him on!"

To applause, Teena happily went on to describe the attorney's physical pluses while another woman drew from the vase. Three more plucked business cards out of The Boot, too, before it was Tam's turn.

"Last draw today," Julia Nguyen said. "Tamara, you can take a card and put it back during the week, if you want. We always keep The Boot on the table, okay?"

"Just go for it," Milla Page said, smiling at her from across the room.

"What can it hurt?" added Mercedes Estevez.

Danica gave Tam a supportive nudge.

New friends, new experiences, a way to get out of the house, maybe even an entertaining time with someone....

What the hell.

Taking a deep breath, Tam stuck her hand inside the vase, grappled around, then came out with a card.

"Julia Nguyen?" Tam said, confused at seeing the woman's name embossed on the thick paper.

"I had to use my own business card," she said, clearly excited to have her recommended man in the spotlight. "Turn it over for my note."

Tam did, hardly surprised to find an organized bulleted list of attributes. She read them out loud. "'Gorgeous gray-blue eyes. Charmer. Dark hair that curls at the ends. Sexy. Waiter. Free spirit.'"

Free spirit. Could he show her the way? Tam's pulse started to thump.

"He was young," Julia said. "Late twenties, I think, and not what you would call successful yet. He's a waiter, but talked about owning his own place a lot. When I saw that he didn't have a card, that told me where he is in life, and it's not where I need a man to be. Still, very, *very*—"

Teena interrupted. "She wouldn't throw him outta bed for eatin' crackers."

Bumpity-bump. Tam's heart wouldn't shut up.

She would be in charge of this one, right? If she could just go into it with no expectations, she could relax and have a little fun.

What did she have to lose?

She glanced at the handwritten name and number on the card: "Kyle Sullivan. Work number: 555-8375."

Her baby step into freedom.

LATER THAT AFTERNOON, a hop skip and a jump away in Union Square, Murphy Sullivan sat at a table in Amidala, the hottest new restaurant from Chef Miike. Known for his experimental Japanese-French fusion dishes, the chef had a cooking show on The Food Channel as well as an avid following of tourists and locals alike. The menu was cutting edge and so was the decor: dark, shiny, modern furniture with avant-garde paintings and sculptures. The main dining room was tinted with chic *Blade Runner*-style touches, the bar lit by low, soft-blue lighting.

Now, an hour before opening, Murphy thought the clientele wouldn't have recognized the atmosphere.

Instead of seeing waiters, busboys and bartenders shined to a polish in their white jackets and black ties, they would've found a group of loud, raucous poker enthusiasts gathered around a linen-clad table, shouting and joking with each other. This was the time to let go—the hour before the sun began to set and the jackets would have to be buttoned. This was the time for the boys to be boys and not automatons who existed to serve.

"Well, kiss my ass!" one of the waiters yelled to the rest of the table as he slammed down his cards. "Full house!"

Murphy, the head bartender here, glanced up from the law brief he'd brought with him. He was proofing it for his day job clerking at his cousin's firm of Doyle, Flynn and Sullivan—not that it did much good in this racket.

"You lookin' over here, Murph?" the waiter with the winning hand asked, his black hair ruffled and his gray-blue eyes wide and teasing. Murphy's cousin, Kyle. "I just leveled these kids. How about you come on over here to get some of that?"

Grinning, Murphy leaned back in his chair, in no hurry to move, letting his laconic attitude speak for itself.

"Aw, come on." Kyle gathered the cards while another waiter stood behind him, marking down how much Kyle had won. "You're the only one around here who gives me a run for my money."

"I'm working."

"Forget about that. You didn't pass the bar last time, so why do you think the results are gonna be any different this time and, *furthermore,* that it'll get you ahead at the firm?"

Some of the staff oohed, as if there was about to be

a big street brawl. Murphy merely shook his head, seemingly amused.

Truthfully, Kyle's words cut into him, made him anxious. He couldn't say why. Murphy had a law degree and valuable experience at the firm under his belt; he wasn't so much afraid he wouldn't pass the bar this time than...what?

Damn, he didn't want to think about what came afterward: hiring on with his cousin Ian's law firm just as he'd always been expected to do. Going to the stifling parties, like the masquerade he'd have to attend this Sunday to network. Having the rest of his life planned out because he couldn't let down his family by doing otherwise.

He sniffed as an enticing aroma—Chef Miike's scallops with mushrooms over rice noodles—wafted past. Murphy closed his eyes, savoring more than just the scent. He held on to a fantasy that had no place on the path he was following—the dream of a restaurant where he could make magic in the kitchen.

As the smell disappeared, he opened his eyes again, seeing the words on the legal brief scattered before him.

Nerves rustled just under his skin, and his heart started to pound. There it was again—pressure building in him, around him, threatening from all sides. He felt as if there was a slab of rock pressing on his chest, pinning him down, stealing his freedom. He'd give his left arm to get out from under it.

But, true to form, Murphy told himself to let it go. Then he put on that carefree attitude like a cloak by resting his hands on the back of his neck, reclining farther in the chair and smiling at Kyle in a who-gives-a-crap way.

He knew it would drive his cousin nuts.

"Look at him," Kyle said lightly, shuffling the cards and grinning at his friends. "The great hope of the Sullivans. The big brain who almost broke the bank to go to law school at fancy-pants Tulane."

Hey, Murphy thought, he and his parents had worked long and hard to get him to the Louisiana college where he'd stayed with relatives, relied on scholarships and worked part-time to make ends meet. Murphy had even delayed enrollment a couple of years after high school graduation just to help earn his way through the school where all the Sullivan lawyers had gone. No wonder he felt so much pressure now. All the cash and hope that had been invested in him made passing the bar and succeeding that much more important.

Going to Tulane held symbolic significance in the family. The first Sullivan brothers had settled in New Orleans during the late 1800s and, gradually, after working their way up the lace-curtain ranks, two descendents had realized their dreams of opening a law practice in 1938. Having been educated at Tulane, they established a family scholarship fund for future Sullivan lawyers, thereby creating a precedent for each generation to aspire to. Sullivans who'd branched out to different areas of the country vied with each other to win the honor of attending the school, and when Murphy had made his parents proud by earning the award, the last thing he'd thought to do was refuse it or question whether it was actually the best school for him.

And while in New Orleans, he'd discovered cooking. Discovered that maybe being a lawyer wasn't his first wish, after all.

Not that it mattered now. Murphy's life was set, and he knew how lucky he was to have fate give him such an opportunity. After graduation, he'd moved back to San Fran to be near his close-knit family and work at his cousin Ian's side, and all was well. For the most part.

Simmering with a low-burning frustration that seemed to get hotter each day, Murphy still didn't let on that Kyle was getting to him. He just leaned back a little farther in that chair.

Kyle glanced over, gauging his cousin's reaction. Not getting much of one, he shook his head and started dealing. When the maître d', Gordon, cruised by the poker table, the waiter keeping track of the bets and winnings casually put the notepad behind his back.

"I've told you," Gordon said, pointing at the cards, "no gambling here."

Eyes wide, Kyle grinned, holding up his hands with the undealt cards still in them. "Who sees any money or poker chips, Gordie? We're playing for *fun*."

Gordon bristled, mostly because the nickname "Gordie" was beneath him. He stiffly walked away, his lips pursed.

Kyle and his comrades laughed as he finished dealing and the waiter took the scratch pad out again. One of the players, the only waitress on staff, verbally anted up while the amounts were recorded.

"Murphy," she said in a deep smoker's voice, "you've got to tell your cousin to kiss up more to Gordon."

"Ah, Murphy doesn't know the meaning of 'kiss' these days," Kyle said, arranging his cards. "The poor boy hasn't had any tail in—what is it now, Murphy? A millennium?"

At the keen reminder, pent-up steam whistled

through Murphy's veins. It'd been a few months, all right—ones that he'd tried to help pass with long days at the firm and the consolation prize of ambition.

Frustrated, Murphy finally stood and sauntered to the card table, glancing over another player's shoulder. The waiter motioned for Murphy to keep his spot while he ran to the john. It was understood that he was trusting levelheaded Murphy to play out his hand without going overboard.

"Kyle's going to grow up one day," Murphy said, assuming the seat, "and leave the playground mentality behind."

His cousin held up a finger. "Youth is wasted on those who don't realize they're gonna get old *real* quick."

As Murphy got rid of two cards, he looked at Kyle. Looked at him closely.

They could've come out of the same womb, he and his cousin. People often commented on how much they resembled each other, even down to their athletic builds and their low voices. But they were so different it spun Murphy's head around. Only two years separated them— Kyle was twenty-seven and he was twenty-nine—but it felt like a lifetime.

Oddly enough, Murphy kind of envied Kyle his outlook—his *carpe diem* nature and big dreams. Trouble was, Kyle never *did* anything to reach his potential, and that's where Murphy stopped wishing he could be just a little more like his cousin.

"So, tell me, genius," Kyle said, dealing the rest of the cards out, "you coming out with us after work tonight or what?"

Murphy kept a smile to himself when he saw that he'd gotten a straight flush. "Got things to do."

"Right, researching some case or another for the underdogs of justice." Cocky as ever, Kyle laid down three jacks. He addressed the other waiters. "I think Murphy just needs to be shanghaied outside his brain long enough for the girls to fall at his feet."

Unbidden heat growled deep inside Murphy. The agony of needing to be inside a wet, warm woman clawed and burned.

He finally laid out his cards, leaning back in his chair again. Kyle's face flushed at his cousin's victory, a muscle in his jaw ticking. But then, after pushing aside the split second of tension, he laughed.

"Just like always," he said, "Murphy's the man."

When Kyle sent him one last glance, Murphy could read everything in it, just as if Kyle was revealing a hand on the table: competitiveness and the longing of a young kid who'd followed Murphy around worshipfully while they'd grown up on the pavements of the Sunset District.

Murphy held his cousin's gaze for a moment before Kyle shook his head then glanced away.

Why did it have to be like this between them? What was this intensity that had defined their relationship since Kyle and his sisters had lost their parents and moved in with Murphy's family so many years ago?

He wished things could change. A lot of things, starting with having to wake up early and go to the firm.

Little did he know that when the head waiter came over to tell Kyle that he had a phone call on the main line, Murphy's wishes would be answered.

Just not in the way he expected.

2

It was Friday night, and Tam's stomach churned with nerves as she sat in a Mandarin-inspired lounge in North Beach, waiting for Kyle Sullivan. A hard-edged song flavored with Chinese lyrics rose above the clatter of an ever-growing crowd as people poured into the red, drag-on-studded room.

"He's still not here," Tam said into her cell phone.

On the other end of the line, Danica's calm voice soothed her. "It's not seven o'clock yet. You've still got ten minutes, so don't sweat it."

Knowing she was right, Tam tugged nervously at her outfit. She'd chosen to wear a flowy black tunic with a raised collar. The sleeves were long, wide, dramatic in their flare, her pants tight and black and mostly covered by a large scarf tied at her hips and covering her rear. The boots were her favorite part, a stretch of leather that came to above her knees—artistic in a pirate kind of way. She wondered if Kyle would like her clothes, if they made a statement, announcing her creative side. If they would run the usual interference for her tonight; provide the usual distraction.

Or maybe he'd think they were dopey. Maybe her even being here was dopey. A mistake. Yup, she'd made a *big* mistake calling this guy, getting all dressed up and going out on the town. Sure, he'd been amused by the whole business-card-in-The-Boot story when she'd called him, and he'd been very charming on the phone, but… Tam's nerves fluttered.

Okay, he'd been downright seductive, with his low, slightly lilting tone, his teasing banter. In Tam's mind, she'd already built him up to be a sex god, a carefree soul who mirrored the person she imagined herself being. As they'd small-talked, her skin had warmed with anticipation.

Had she finally found a guy who'd be on her same wavelength, even if it was for just a lighthearted, confidence-inspiring fling?

An actual date, she kept thinking. I told him I was looking for a good time. That means I might actually get to feel a man's hands on me again.…

She blew out a breath.

"You just relax," Danica said. "That's exactly what *I'm* doing, waiting for my workaholic lawyer here at the bar in Rubicon. Spiffy, huh? He insisted on paying for dinner here. Got to be pretty well off—not that I'm shallow enough to have that be a prime requirement or anything. Still…*bonus!*"

Tam couldn't help laughing at her friend's bubbly nature. "I just hope we don't end up on my couch at midnight, eating from a tub of Rocky Road and telling each other war stories."

"Good times, that's all that's in store for you. Wait. This might be him. I think he sees the red rose I told him I'd have."

At the mention of the "marker"—a symbol that

would allow one blind date to recognize the other—Tam clutched hers, too. She'd told Kyle Sullivan that she'd be holding a black-and-silver Japanese fan. It complemented her outfit and gave her nervous hands something to do with themselves.

"Good luck," Tam said.

"Good luck to you, too. Go get him!" And with that, Danica was gone.

Tam was left to sit alone at her high table near the wall, her eye on the door as she anxiously awaited her own date: the man with the gray-blue eyes and black hair The Boot had promised.

As KYLE AND MURPHY ambled down the sidewalk toward the lounge, Kyle patted Murphy on the back.

"You should've heard her on the phone," he said. "Sexy, sweet and just looking for trouble. Damn, I hope she's as gorgeous as she sounds."

The words were like white noise, simple to ignore. As usual, Kyle had been on Murphy all week, yapping and yapping about how Murphy needed to come out with him on their night off and meet some women.

And, since there was only so much temptation Murphy could take, he'd reached his limit a few hours ago, finally giving in. It'd been much too easy. His whole body was on complete overload, screaming to ease the physical ache that too much work and not enough play had inspired.

Yet…good Lord. Murphy *knew* how this adventure with Kyle would go. While his cousin romanced his blind date, Murphy might meet an interesting woman, talk to her, buy her a few drinks, but then the old con-

science would kick in and he'd convince himself that
he needed to get back to work.

He wouldn't enjoy himself. He didn't know how.

Just thinking about it made Murphy want to tear
something apart. Why did he constantly hold himself on
such a tight leash? With the encouragement of parents
who'd had to scrape by all their lives, he'd always been
too intent on making something of himself and fighting
off the distractions that threatened to hold him back.
Even his ex-girlfriends had complained about his reluc-
tance to deviate from anything but work, work, work.

Despite his mental detour, Murphy could still hear
Kyle talking, could still catch a whiff of his cousin's aft-
ershave. It hovered over the aroma of garlic that wafted
out of a corner Italian trattoria.

"Tamara Clarkson made sure I knew she's ready to
roll," Kyle continued. "Just my type. And we'll find you
a sure thing tonight, too, huh?"

"It's not like my johnson needs a nanny," Murphy
said dryly. "I've got this under control."

"Control?" Kyle gave Murphy a slight, taunting
push. "The point is to lose control, Mr. Button-Down."

Right, Murphy thought. Kyle was right.

They were approaching the door, into which a cluster
of young tourists, probably from nearby Fisherman's
Wharf, disappeared.

"Here goes," Kyle said. He smoothed down his hair,
which had a tendency to go untamed if he didn't watch
it. "Now turn on the charm, Murph. I know you're that
strong and silent type, but sometimes girls like to be acknowledged with actual conversation."

"Just get in there, Lothario."

"I'll do my best not to break any hearts—" Murphy's cousin paused at the threshold, where hard music spilled into the twilight "—unless I have to."

Kyle flashed Murphy a smile and stepped inside, immediately glancing around the room and becoming a part of the crowd.

A master of the game, Murphy thought, keeping Kyle within his line of sight as he sauntered into the thick of the mob, too. *Just look at him, an expert on the prowl.* He knew how to make women happy, even if he wasn't very good at letting them down easy after the fun was done.

Kyle's other weak point was his pickiness. He was a dog when it came to wanting only the gorgeous and lean sorority thoroughbreds who were ready to roll. And if they didn't strike him as attractive right away, he tended to lose interest and move on to the next conquest. At the moment Kyle was sticking to the shadows of the room, searching for his date, wanting to check her out before committing.

That was his modus operandi, Murphy thought. Just a big enthusiastic kid who hadn't grown up to appreciate more than a pretty face.

He shook his head and glanced away. If he had his younger cousin's lust for life, he would use it wisely. But that was the whole point—Kyle *wasn't* wise. He lived in the moment, out from under the weight of responsibility.

So, deep down, why did Murphy yearn to be that way, too?

Strains of a Chinese rock ballad tore through the room, ripping into Murphy and exacerbating his physical need with every vibration. Scenes from a Jet

Li movie flashed over the TV screens hovering in the corners, the images stylized with vengeance and blood.

Murphy's pulse pushed through him, awakening him. He missed being with people. Missed the friction of nearby bodies, the murmur of voices, the scent of a woman's shampoo as she brushed by him.

He headed for the bar, the crowd around it as thick as collected moss, their bodies emanating heat. Impatient for a drink, Murphy looked around, deciding to get his social poison from a waitress instead.

And that's when he saw her.

At a distant table, a woman waited, clutching a fan in one fist. The first personal feature Murphy noticed was her hair—a wild Bohemian bunch of light-brown curls that spilled down to her shoulders. Her fan, her hair, even the way she leaned on the table with her chin in her palm while playing with a corkscrewed strand, added up to a certain dramatic quirkiness.

Just as he was about to admit that she wasn't anywhere near his type—a female who carried ambition in the disciplined cut of her hair and the steel of her posture suited him much better—he noticed this woman's eyes. They were a startling blue, widened with such emotion—anxiety?—that he couldn't look away. Eyes flashing with intelligent awareness, drawing Murphy in.

It was only when she blinked, then glanced at the door, that he noticed the off-kilter black clothing, the long boots hugging her legs, which were crossed, one ankle bobbing in time to the slow, revving guitar licks of the stereo.

Lust blindsided him, twisting in his belly, heating downward until his gut tightened.

Those boots. In spite of everything else about her, they made her into one of those bad girls Kyle had been tempting him with, a woman who'd do anything—with her mouth, with her hands and with her body.

Murphy craved a woman with such boots.

For a long second he allowed himself to wallow in the thought of her, to bathe himself in the mist of wicked longing.

He imagined slipping those boots off her legs or…damn, even keeping them *on* as he ran his thumbs over the inside of her thighs…. Somehow, with the deftness only a fantasy would allow, he could keep those boots on while working off her pants and underwear—which would be black lace, of course—and then parting those legs so he could see all of her.

She'd give him a naughty smile, her mouth lush with that shiny pink gloss she was wearing, then crook her finger at him.

Come on. What're you waiting for?

He'd go to her, using his fingers to spread her apart. Her sex would be a deep pink, swollen, already wet. When he tasted her, she'd be warm, his tongue playing around the hood of her clit, teasing it, dipping inside her, kissing her until she moved against his mouth, asking for more, needing it, wanting it…

Asking him to punish this bad, bad girl with the pain of pleasure.

A loud laugh from behind Murphy shook him back to the moment.

He realized he was in a bar, in a crowd, and his cock was aching with fierce, stiff electricity.

Hell, the fantasy had been good while it'd lasted.

He glanced back at the woman, who was now stirring her drink, looking into its depths as if she could read the ice like tea leaves. He wanted to fixate on those boots again, but he couldn't. Not this time.

Because in this second glance he saw something else about her—a sadness? Something almost hidden under the unruly hair, something that made her hold his attention for a few seconds longer than a girl would who was so obviously not his style.

But his body wasn't about to let him get away with that. His penis was nudging against his jeans, still awake.

Great. In the middle of a crowd—the perfect place for an emerging hard-on.

It was at that well-timed moment of frustration that she glanced up, meeting the intensity of his gaze.

She sat up in her chair, smiled, the gesture full of cheer and hope, and the room's temperature rose about fifty degrees.

He couldn't explain why, but his pulse jerked, and it wasn't from animal need this time. Seeing her all alone like this and smiling at him jiggered some kind of switch, merging desire and emotion into a confusing brew.

As he stood there, body raging, *keening,* his cell phone rang. It vibrated against a region that really didn't require any more encouragement.

Blood pounding, he calmed himself and broke eye contact with the woman, answering the call.

But he couldn't hear anything, so he headed for the door, managing to get there even with the state of his union rubbing against his jeans.

Kyle was waiting for him outside. Murphy knew

his cousin too well—this wasn't a good sign for the blind date.

"You can hang up. It's just me." Kyle tucked his own phone into his pocket, pulling Murphy away from the building and down the street.

"Hold up," Murphy said, shoving his own phone away. He grabbed his cousin's arm and stopped him from walking any farther. "Tell me you're not ditching your date."

Kyle guided Murphy near the entrance of a closed bakery, the enclosure partially hiding them. "I don't need to be a fortuneteller to see that there's nothing there."

"You didn't even have time to talk to her, so how could you know that? Isn't she enough of a babe for you, Kyle?"

Murphy didn't even know why he was firing away with these questions when the answers were so obvious. This was how Kyle operated; the process was no surprise.

Kyle flinched at Murphy's tone, telling Murphy that he'd hit every target.

"She didn't live up to what I pictured," Kyle said. "The reality killed the fantasy, that's all."

"Perfect. Good from far, but far from good."

"Cut it out, Murphy, I'll call her right now to say I've got an urgent situation and can't make it. That way neither of us will waste our time by pretending something'll come of this. No harm done." Kyle socked Murphy in the arm. "Then we'll be on our way to better things, because my guy Murphy needs some distraction."

Adding to his roguish act, Kyle offered a grin, but Murphy was immune.

"What?" Kyle asked, stuffing his hands in his pockets. He leaned against the building, watching a group of suntanned girls in light dresses walk by. Oddly enough, he didn't even smile as they said hi to him. Instead he gave a slight nod, then fixed a lowered, tentative gaze on his cousin.

"Hell," Murphy said, "at least you've got standards. At least you won't screw anything that walks, right?"

Kyle exhaled, clearly relieved that Murphy had gotten his point. "Exactly. Why even make her think there's a possibility of—"

"You're a real hero, saving her feelings like this." Murphy grunted. "You're so damned shallow that you make a trickle of water look deep."

"Well, shit, you want to go back in there and go on this mercy date instead? Be my guest. Tamara Clarkson's the one with the frizzed-out hair, sitting in the corner with a weird fan. Go for it."

Murphy's head almost crashed in on itself. His still-awakened groin stirred. "A fan?"

"Yeah, a fan. Among other things, I'm not into average Josies from the drama club."

Anger—odd and unexplained—welled up in Murphy. "I saw her. She was…" He stopped himself, but his mind finished the thought. She wasn't average. Hell, no. Striking, yes. A stroke of color in a roomful of moving nothings. A woman who didn't fit any traditional mold—not society's definition of beauty, anyway. How could Kyle think she was average?

"Listen." Murphy leaned closer, offended for her. "I know how you play it. You sweet-talked her on the phone, got her hopes up, and now you'll drop her without another care. She's probably going to be crushed that you stood her up."

"You feel sorry for her."

Hell, yeah, he did. But it was more than that. It was disappointment in Kyle's lack of maturity. A twinge of jealousy, because Kyle always seemed to get what Murphy wanted with such relaxed ease—and took it all for granted.

Freedom. Careless immunity from accountability.

Murphy got angrier just thinking about it. Angry with himself for wanting the same thing.

But there was also something else—something much more disturbing about leaving Tamara Clarkson alone in the lounge. She'd *seen* Murphy, brightened at the sight of him. Based on how alike the cousins looked, she'd thought he was Kyle, didn't she? Murphy might as well be the one ditching her for all she knew, and that didn't sit right with him. Not at all.

Ironic, huh? He would love to go back in there, to talk with her and see where things led, to be Kyle for just one night, but he couldn't.

"If she'd been *my* date…" Murphy said, trailing off.

"You'd what?" Kyle said, challenging him.

Images ran through his head: boots, skin-on-skin, sighs…

But the good guy in Murphy shut the fantasy machine down in the face of taking care of business. As usual.

Still, his body throbbed, unrelenting in its desire.

"I'd do the right thing," Murphy finished, the words flavorless and drab, not halfway near what he would really like to say. "Tell me, what's so wrong with spending an hour with her? Just one goddamned hour?"

"It's not that. It's…" Kyle ran a hand through his short dark hair. "I hate seeing the look on their faces when things don't go the way they want them to, you know? The disappointment. I don't like making them feel that way."

"How sensitive. Why don't you just forget about this and go on to another bar where you can meet a girl who suits your discriminating appetites? In the meantime, I'll go back inside and make some excuse to Tamara Clarkson. I'll buy her that drink you owe her."

"You don't need—"

"I think I do." He detailed how Tamara had seen him and how that made Murphy feel responsible. "I'm not going to stand by and watch while you make this woman's night a disaster."

"Murphy…"

Kyle seemed devastated by his cousin's disgust. Murphy knew the look: it was that of a little brother who'd disappointed the older sibling he idolized. But Murphy was hurting, too, because he'd always hoped that his younger cousin was better than this. Yet every time Murphy realized it wasn't true, it pained him that much more.

"Are you really going to take over my date?" Kyle asked, seeming half relieved, half chastised.

"Damn straight. In fact, Kyle, maybe I'll just go in there and pretend I'm *you,* just like you suggested," he said, not meaning it. "Because you primed her for that wild man she talked to on the phone and I'm not him. Wouldn't it be ironic if I got dumped because *I* wasn't what *she* wanted?"

When Kyle raised his eyebrows, Murphy made a

dismissive gesture, fighting off a strange thrust of yearning. He'd meant to be ridiculous, to mock his cousin, but the words were still hanging in the air.

She wanted a wild man. She wanted Kyle.

A flame licked at the inside of his belly. Murphy had thought about how great it would be to assume Kyle's identity, just for the night. To walk freely and shove aside all his hang-ups. To play out the fantasies he'd entertained while watching her inside that lounge.

Stupid idea, Murphy thought. Crazy.

"Just… God, get out of here," Murphy said, pissed off at Kyle. At himself.

"But—"

"*Go.*"

At Murphy's derisive command, Kyle started to walk away, glancing back over his shoulder at his cousin. He looked like a stray dog who'd been kicked to the curb by the owner he adored. Then he disappeared around the corner, shoulders slumped.

Murphy fisted his hands, battling an urge to catch up to Kyle and take back his harsh words. But he couldn't. Not when the ego of that woman was at stake. Not when it was up to Murphy to take care of her now.

Take care of her.…

As he stood there, excitement took root, even as he told himself that usurping Kyle's place didn't mean anything more than buying a beautiful, desirable woman one drink…even as he fought the feeling that she would be disappointed with getting a mild man instead of a wild man.

IT WAS 7:20.

Tam wanted to go home, but she also wanted to wait

for Kyle Sullivan—if that's who the guy had been—to come back into the bar. If he *was* her blind date, had he run as far away and as fast as he could after getting one look at her?

Middle-school-bred insecurities rushed back to her—long face, long nose…horse face.

She didn't want to think about it. But he'd booked out of the lounge pretty quickly with that cell phone to his ear and hadn't returned.

The reminder made her feel lonelier than ever, kicking her into departure mode. A hole numbed her stomach, an empty place where she could hide the ugly truth: he'd thought she wasn't pretty. Her clothes, her determination to look approachable, hadn't worked.

Stinging, she reached for her small shoulder bag. Then she headed for the door, telling herself that she was fine, chalking the night up to just another crummy day in the jungle. A day that would probably set her back another year in the dating department but—what the hell—she'd get over it.

Eventually.

But as she threaded her way to the door, she stopped in her tracks.

Because there he was, standing not five feet away, gazing at the table she'd deserted. Three college girls had already claimed the space, giggling and offering each other cheers at their good fortune.

He put his hands on his hips, turning around, surveying the room, and…

Oh. My. God.

Tam's heartbeat thundered in her head. If this was her date, he'd lived up to the advertisement, with those blue-gray eyes that were more gorgeous than she could've ever imagined. Dark eyebrows winged above them, lending him a wry edge. He also had the promised black hair, cut short, conservative, although she did sense a hint of wildness where the strands had grown out, showing a bit of curl. He was tall and well built. A T-shirt covered a wide chest, muscles roping through his arms.

Very, *very* hot. So hot she wondered how long he would talk to her before realizing he was too hot to *be* talking to her.

Should she go to him and find out if he was her guy?

She heard a group of voices in the back of her mind. The Sisters of the Booty Call, their chant rising in power: *Do it, do it, do it…*

If not now, when? She was here to take control, right?

Sucking in a breath, she forced her body in his direction, walking with determination.

All too soon she was standing in front of him, her heart jittering against her ribs.

"Looking for this?" she said, flashing her fan.

Was that her sounding all flirty and confident again? See, she could cover what she'd been feeling only moments ago. And why not? She'd spent most of a lifetime being good at it.

When he spun around, spotted the date marker and grinned in acknowledgment, she almost tumbled to the floor.

Oh. My. God. Part two.

That smile…it was aimed at her. *Her.* Tamara Clarkson, the girl who, only moments ago, thought her date had burned rubber.

Over the music, he motioned toward an empty spot near the wall, gently grabbing her elbow to lead her. Her skin blazed against the pressure of his fingers, a bolt of electricity zigzagging down through her tummy, just about splitting her apart, leaving her aching.

"I had some difficulty getting back in here," he said, battling the music with his voice. "Sorry about keeping you waiting."

See, everything was okay. In fact, he was leaning against the plank wall, aiming his body toward her, giving her an appreciative glance that made her skin flush.

"Want a drink?" she asked boldly.

Go, girl, go, girl…

He paused, sending a flash of terror into her chest. But then he seemed to consider something, and he broke into that sexy, slow smile.

"What'll you have?" he asked, his eyebrows raising suggestively.

Whoo-boy. Tam knew what she wanted.

3

UP CLOSE, her eyes were breathtaking.

Clear and open. The touch of innocence he glimpsed in them made him wonder if she knew what wearing a pair of thigh-high boots did to a guy.

He felt himself stirring to life again, a clutch of welcome agony that had a hold of his cock and wouldn't let go.

As he watched Tamara Clarkson order a Mai Tai, he concentrated on her pouty mouth, drawn by every word she formed while she talked. All he wanted was reach out to trace her lips with his fingers, to slip one inside and slide it in and out as a promise, an invitation.

How would she react if he tried it? He could tell she was attracted to him, but maybe that was because she'd already talked to Kyle and he'd pumped her up with expectations Murphy couldn't even begin to think of fulfilling. Or could he?

He realized that Tamara was staring at him. Had she asked a question that he'd been too hot and bothered to hear?

Recovering more smoothly than he could ever have anticipated, he pretended that the music and the crowd's noise had been the problem. He leaned over to her, closer.

As she laughed a little, her warm breath caressed his ear. And even over the bar's working-class perfume of stale sweat and hops, he caught the scent of her: honeysuckle and orange blossoms, earthy and sweet.

Murphy's skin flared with a flash of heat.

"I thought maybe you'd changed your mind and left." She paused, bit her bottom lip then smiled. "I thought that…well, maybe you decided the business-card routine was too forward after all, too out of the ordinary. But then I remembered what you said on the phone.…"

There was a daring gleam in her eyes as she trailed off and backed away from him just enough to gauge his answer, possibly even to ferret out why he *had* left the lounge earlier.

There was no way he would say that Kyle had judged her as "not pretty enough" and abandoned the date for greener pastures.

Searching for an answer, Murphy could only guess what Kyle had already said to her. And whatever the specifics, Tamara Clarkson had clearly liked every bit of Kyle's act. He could tell by the anticipation in the flush of her cheeks, the way her body was angled toward him, as his was toward hers.

Before he could stop himself, he leaned down and said something that could've come straight out of Kyle's own mouth.

"I like knowing that you made the first move." His lips brushed against her hair. "Confidence is attractive, and it shows that you're open to—" he laughed, her strands tickling his mouth "—anything we come up with."

Damn, even his voice sounded like his cousin's. It

wasn't hard to imitate Kyle—his own mom couldn't even tell them apart on the phone—but it was the *tone* he used that rattled him.

The innuendo that he was a different man.

Tamara's fingers were pressed against his chest, not to push him away, but perhaps in reaction to what he'd said. He wondered if she could feel his heart banging, if the vibration of his pulse had traveled through her hand and was echoing inside of her.

Instinct told him that she wanted to hear more of Kyle's flirting, that she might already be so into the fantasy of Kyle that she might reject Murphy if he backtracked and told her who he really was.

A boring drone. A turnoff to someone with Tamara's obvious predilection for a wild boy.

Was telling the truth worth it when things were going so well? What would revealing his identity accomplish, especially since this wasn't going to turn into a serious relationship anyway? After tonight, she would never be the wiser to his identity, especially if Murphy could use to his advantage all the persuasive skills he'd professionally honed and somehow convince her that a single date would be enough, that it would be *her* idea never to see him again. Could he manage that?

It was a hell of a lot better than what Kyle would've done.

Going beyond tonight with her wasn't an option, anyway. The less she knew, the more likely it was that she would never find out why Kyle had unceremoniously dumped her. Murphy didn't wish that truth on any woman.

She turned her face so that she was talking near his

ear again. "You're my first date in this city. I don't know much about what to do for kicks."

"You're in my capable hands."

They grinned at each other, the double entendre hardly lost on either of them. In that moment, he realized that she *did* know what her boots were all about. That she'd worn them on purpose. That she hadn't been kidding about having a good time when she'd talked to Kyle on the phone.

As the waitress brought their drinks, Murphy insisted on paying, not only because it was courteous but because he wanted to make this up to her. He was lying by omission, and he felt too good to stop.

He took a swig of the draft beer, and she sipped from her cocktail. The drink left some moisture on her lower lip, and she sucked at it, casting him a slanted look.

He leaned close again, breathing her in, feeling drunk with the freedom of stepping outside of himself, of playing a naughty game that had no rules.

"What do you like to do, Tamara Clarkson?"

Definitely Kyle: teasing, lightly charming, the kind of guy women forgave a few lies because he was so entertaining.

"The usual." She stirred her drink, ice-sweat clinging to the glass. "Travel, read, watch too much TV." She made an endearingly goofy face. "I decorate stuff, too."

"Decorate?"

When she laughed, his neck tingled with the dampness of her breath. It smelled of exotic fruits.

"I'm working on some home improvements. And I kind of have this thing for making my own clothes.

Fashion makes the world—" she paused, shrugged "—a more beautiful place, I suppose."

He ran a lingering gaze over her body, from the high neck of the wide-sleeved, gauzy blouse, over her breasts, down her scarf-clad waist, past her hips to her legs.

She shifted, as if restless under the weight of his lazy perusal. Just like that he was turned on again, his entire body one beating mass of erotic energy.

At that moment, it became perfectly clear to Murphy: what he wanted more than anything in this world was for her to desire him, to surrender to his hands as they roamed her up and down, to ask for more as he peeled off the layers of clothing that separated them.

Primal, predatory. His lust robbed him of logic. All that existed was here and now. *Want. Need.*

"You're talented," he said, voice ragged as he dragged his gaze back to her face. "You really know how to dress, Tamara."

"Tam," she said, voice soft in his ear. "Just Tam, okay?"

Heartbeats marked the seconds that thudded between them.

Murphy propped his arm on the wall, just below the gold of a Chinese symbol. With him hovering over her, she had to tilt her chin to look up at him.

She wasn't a short woman, coming up to just above his shoulder. Their proximity meant that her mouth was *this* close to his neck. All she would have to do is cant over a couple of inches to press her lips to his skin.

The music's volume abruptly lowered, breaking the flow of his thoughts. With a glance, Murphy discovered that the bartender had turned down the stereo while he argued with a patron who'd imbibed way too much happy juice.

Great. That meant there was no need to lean over her anymore. The lack of a rhythmic, driving cadence changed the room's tone, somehow set them back to first-date distance.

"Julia had nice things to say about you." Tam was holding her drink in front of her chest now.

Kyle. She was talking about Kyle. Murphy had to keep reminding himself.

"What did Julia have to say?" Murphy asked, not certain who the woman even was. Could she be the one who'd put Kyle's name into the business-card lottery? His cousin had told him all about the setup, but had failed to mention the name of the lady he'd impressed, not that he probably even remembered.

"Hmm, let me think. What *did* she say?" Tam tapped a finger against her mouth, stopped, then glanced at him sideways out of the corner of her eye.

Cute. Taunting him, huh?

Murphy inched nearer, lowering his arm from the wall.

"Tell me everything," he said, tweaking a curl that was hanging down to her collarbone. Inadvertently—or maybe not—he skimmed against the thin material separating his finger from her flesh, and her face went red.

Strangely, it was the most seductive reaction he could've wished for. An unexpected combination, an angel wearing the devil's lingerie.

"You going to hold me in suspense here?" he asked. "Or are you going to tell me what Julia said?"

"Oh, just the basics."

She tentatively reached out, tugged on the bottom of his T-shirt. It was the shy move of an unpracticed hand, confusing Murphy. Stoking him further.

"She said you're a waiter," she added, "but you want to open your own restaurant someday."

Murphy wasn't sure how to respond. He and Kyle *had* talked about this, but never seriously. His cousin didn't have the ambition to commit to that kind of project. But it was true that Murphy loved the dream of his own place, where he could indulge himself in the world's second-best stress-relieving activity: cooking. Kyle enjoyed it just as much, meaning that it was one more thing for them to get competitive over.

Also, Murphy wasn't Kyle, and the reminder sent another ping of adrenaline through him.

Forget it. All he knew was that he wanted to be touching her again, and from the way she kept glancing at him from beneath her eyelashes, he guessed that she felt the same way.

When she opened her mouth to say something else, Murphy impetuously took up where she'd left off when she'd pulled at his T-shirt. He casually ran a finger down her thinly covered arm, just as if he did this sort of thing every night of the week. Her mouth remained open, the words frozen as she watched his face.

The breath caught in his chest while he waited for her reaction.

HIS TOUCH BURNED her world at its edges.

As Tam stood there, stunned and overjoyed, she heard the sucking sound of flame being pulled into her body—a backdraft that singed through her flesh, deeper, until it flared around her belly, stirring her up and making her keenly aware of how badly she'd missed being with a man.

Driving home how much she wanted *this* man.

The awakening interest she'd felt for him on the phone was nothing compared to what was happening now—the fire, the attraction, the utter pleasure of connecting.

He was measuring her with an intense gaze, tacitly asking her to come a step closer to what she'd been hoping for when she'd drawn his name out of the vase.

For a good time call...

But just as she was about to respond—with a gesture? with words?—a stumbling girl backed into Tam, making her cocktail splash over her glass's rim and onto her hand.

Immediately Kyle reached out to keep the tanked girl from knocking into Tam again.

"You all right?" he asked Tam.

The party girl cut off her response, grabbing on to Kyle's arm and swaying into him.

"Whoa. Will you marry me?" she asked, slurring.

Her friends broke into embarrassed laughter and dragged her away. Clearly amused, Kyle raised his eyebrows and shrugged.

Was he flushing a little? Nah. Couldn't be. Based on what she'd already learned about Kyle Sullivan, he wouldn't be the type. Nope—not the cocky man who'd accepted a weird call for a blind date. Not the anything-goes guy who'd offered to show her the ropes tonight.

She blew out a breath, and shrugged. "So much for privacy here."

His eyes widened a little as he handed her a napkin

to dry off. Jeez, she'd sounded…well, really *easy*. Sounded as if she was hot to get him alone.

But wasn't she?

Before she could find an answer, he was back to making her feel like the most beautiful woman in the room, giving her that teasing look, that knowing smile.

"Want to get out of this zoo?" he asked.

He was into her! She held back a happy dance.

"That'd be great. Maybe some fresh air?"

Fresh air. Heh. So that's what they called it these days.

He took her hand, his fingers warm around hers, and led her through the crowd and out of the lounge, into the purple-gray of coming night. The wind had picked up a little, toying with her hair as they headed toward God-knows-where.

"I know a quieter bar nearby," he said, squeezing her hand, not letting go, even though they were done with dodging people.

She liked that he was still holding her, liked that she could link her fingers through his and feel her arm rubbing against those muscles.

They passed boutiques, other bars, a dance club. Soon he slowed their pace, and she felt the urge to chat, because it'd been so simple with him before.

"So. Whereabouts do you live?"

"Over in Sunset. I've got an apartment—"

He cut himself off, then laughed. Did he want to keep this night on an impersonal level? Part of her applauded the decision, but the other part…

Get a grip, she thought. *You're not here to get serious.*

"And you?" he asked.

Odd. She'd told him on the phone. But…whatever. He'd probably forgotten.

"I moved to Russian Hill a few weeks ago." Before he could start with the inevitable commentary, she hurried to correct his admiration. "I'm just house-sitting one of my family's places while my dad is on a long-term consulting job in New York. I'm not exactly a perfect Hill fit, so don't worry."

Clearly, *she* had no reservations about talking too much—especially about why she was living in such a swank location. But that was what she did when she was nervous—cover the awkwardness with chatter.

Her breast brushed against his biceps, and she felt him tense, as if holding himself back.

"How'd you end up in that kind of home?" he asked, voice low, rougher than it had been on the phone, an almost-growl taking the place of the very faint lilt.

When she drew in a breath, it sounded shaky, all her pent-up needs wavering on the edge.

"My dad took a job here back when I was in college. He's an architect and fell in love with the house because it's from the—what is it?" She snapped her fingers. "Second Bay-Area Tradition Style."

Despite the house's beauty, it was lonely living by herself. She concentrated on Kyle's nod to chase away the thought.

"What about your mom?" Kyle asked.

"Divorced. We talk on the phone, but…" She faded off, not wanting to chat about this. To hide it, she perked up, determined to make this night a great one. "Enough about me. You've got a family, I suppose."

"You're not thinking I was raised by wolves? I've given you the wrong impression, then." He grinned down at her, and she could tell by the look on his face that, even during this seduction, he could still allow a moment of affection for his family to intrude.

But seconds later his eyes had darkened again, consuming her as he ran a gaze over her mouth.

Her knees wobbled a bit. Whoo-boy.

She swallowed. "Wolves? Except for the part where you were late, you're a perfect gentleman."

His laugh was on the biting side. He chopped it off by gesturing toward the entrance of a nondescript bar, indicating that this was their destination.

When he ushered her inside, their talk about personal details eased off. That was because she was too enchanted by the room to pursue anything else.

The decor was beatnik, with low lighting, intimate booths and a sense of indelible cool. Two women dressed in Kerouacesque turtlenecks—the only customers—played pool under the multihued liquor bottles that hung from the rafters. The glass was backed by soft lights, creating a rainbow of muted color. Near the back, a door opened into what looked like a courtyard, and next to it, a man worked his fingers over the strings of a bass, his tune moody and sinful.

Kyle grabbed them a couple of drinks, then led her outside where lounge chairs faced an empty wooden stage. They probably held spoken-word readings here, she thought, excited by the prospect. But right now she and Kyle were alone.

She felt his gaze on her, and when she met it, he wasn't smiling anymore.

No. He had that look. The look of a man who'd brought her here for privacy.

She returned that look, ready for whatever came next.

SHE WAS ACTUALLY responding to him.

The confirmation of his hopes only added to the heady thrill of what he was getting away with. For the first time in years, he was breathing easy. In fact, he hadn't even thought of work since Kyle had left, and that was something.

Still…what in the hell was he doing?

He set down their drinks then watched as she sighed and sank back against the brick wall. Beneath the glow of a lantern, the buttery hue bathed her skin, making the highlights in her curly hair dance. Her hand drifted up to touch her neck, and she rubbed her fingertips over her skin, as if sending a silent invitation.

"I've been here during the summer, way back when," he said. "They had a man who spoke Ray Charles songs like they were poems."

The low, alluring musings from the bass floated on the air, seducing his conscience, telling him it was okay to lie for just one night.

"Does he still perform here?" Tam asked. Her voice wasn't higher than a whisper.

"I have no idea. I—" Careful.

He'd almost added that he didn't have much time for entertainment anymore, but he'd stopped himself. Kyle wouldn't have said it, and neither should he.

Suddenly too self-aware, Murphy didn't move toward her, even though he was dying to.

In an effort to change the subject yet again, he said, "Your hair. It's…"

"I know. Messy. Frizzed out."

She glanced away, and disappointment seized him. But then, as if recovering from something, she looked at him again, allowing that huge, gorgeous smile to light over her lips.

"It's not messy at all," he said. "I like it."

Understatement. It reminded him of steamy nights, of a woman lounging on a bed with the sheets sweated to her body, her hair in disarray. Reminded him of younger, New Orleans-misted memories from Tulane.

Dammit, he wanted to see her that way, sated and relaxed by what he could do to her.

"I guess," she said, voice low as she moved closer, "it's natural that you'd like my hair. You said on the phone that you're into wild things."

The comment made him smile. And he knew it was a smile he wouldn't normally wear. It felt wolfish, appropriate for a man reaching out to test a woman's hair between his fingers, wishing he could slip his hand a little lower.…

"You're into the same things, right, Tam?"

She was playing the game—the touch-and-go of verbal foreplay. It was in the tilt of her mouth, the rise of her chin as she met his stare.

"Wild as in…?" she ventured.

Screw it.

He reached toward her, coasting his fingers to the back of her neck, slipping one into her high collar to smooth over her nape. He heard her intake of breath.

"As in—" he whisked his fingertips downward over

her spine to the small of her back, where he started drawing slow circles "—anything goes."

Good. So, so good.

As her breathing got faster, his other hand crept around to her throat. He stoked the soft skin of it, feeling her working to swallow.

"I don't really even know you from Adam," she said.

Or Kyle.

She'd said the right words, revving him up with the reminder that he'd left himself behind.

"Then we need to do something about getting acquainted," he whispered.

He knew she could leave right now—that he could, too. But neither of them was moving.

Maybe she *was* the type of woman who knew what kind of message those boots sent. And maybe she could give Murphy what he needed.

A taste of bad.

4

As Kyle stroked Tam's throat, he also pressed and circled his fingers just below her spine—in very insistent, *very* persuasive caresses. They sent rivulets of gathered steam through her belly, dampening and readying her for more.

Her breathing picked up speed, and she instinctively shifted her hips, getting closer to him. When her stomach brushed his jeans, a hard ridge told her that this was really *on*. That she was back in the game.

She gripped his shirt as her sex tightened into a pinpoint of stimulated pain.

She'd missed this. One whole year had gone by since her last make-out session, but, miraculously, tonight was proving that it wasn't impossible for her to be wanted. How was it that this gorgeous man didn't see what she saw in the mirror?

Still…there was something keeping her from fully grinding against him, giving in and going for it. Was it fear that he would realize he wasn't attracted to her after all?

An excuse, she thought biting her lip and fighting the thoughts that wouldn't leave her alone. *That's just a lie you tell yourself instead of facing the real reasons you're afraid.*

In the back of her mind, she remembered a long-ago night, the aroma of barbecued hamburgers still lingering on the air from dinner. She'd stayed outside in the dry Nevada air to play with some dolls, but her parents had gone in once they'd started arguing again. They'd unwittingly left their bedroom window open.

You screwed him, her dad had said, agonized. *And it wasn't just one time. Didn't you think I'd find out?*

In answer, her mom had only cried.

Now Tam pushed away the memory. But she couldn't deny that this was why she stayed home so many weekend nights. To avoid a relationship that could one day lead to secrets and lies, to a breakup as wounding as her parents'. A divorce that had given her too many reasons to get tired of the dating world quickly and easily. A divorce that had established a pattern for rejection after her mother had abandoned her without a fight.

"Tam," Kyle whispered. His breath was laced with a reminder of the beer he'd had at the last bar.

The word tingled her ear and, with a final refusal to listen to her misgivings, she gave in to the warmth, finding it could be oddly simple to forget everything but him if she allowed herself to. He nuzzled her cheek, his own scratched with stubble. He smelled like shaving cream—clean and masculine.

The scent, the friction of a man's skin on her own, struck a primal chord. She twisted his shirt out of his pants, the vibration of the bass from the main bar throbbing in her ears. Gently she latched her teeth against his neck, tasting the tang of him, and bit lightly.

Kyle grunted, obviously surprised. Then he laughed

softly, sliding a palm under her butt. With determined force, he guided her out of the light and into a corner where the darkness semicovered them from anyone who might wander into the yard.

Oh, yeah, Tam thought, too excited to even think anymore. It's on.

He pressed her back against the brick wall. His arms cushioned her from most of it as he planed his body against hers, fit himself comfortably then—after a second in which they both caught their breath—almost arrogantly. In the next instant, his lips covered hers, wet and carnal. An open-mouthed kiss, it was both demanding and languorous, spinning her mind out of her body and replacing it with pure impulse.

Solid thoughts escaped her, and she saw butterflies on the backs of her eyelids, free and open, within her reach.

Grasping at the liberation, she gave herself over to Kyle's kiss, devouring him right back, threading her fingers through his hair and rubbing her body against his.

His erection had only gotten harder, prodding her as she wrapped a boot-clad leg around him.

He gasped for air, almost as if she'd just thrown a punch at his gut. But he recovered quickly, nibbling at her ear and skimming his hand over her boot. He panted, and in the dimness, she could see him glancing down at her leg. At he same time, he arched into her, made her groan low in her throat.

"These boots…" he said.

At the hint of frantic reverence in his tone, her confidence climbed a notch. "What about them?"

He adjusted his grip on her leg, rocking her against his stiffness at the same time. She made another wincing sound of pleasure. Her sex was slick and pounding with longing—damn, she could hardly stand it.

Expertly, he slid a palm up to the cusp of her boot, inserted a finger into the gape where suede met the cotton of her pants. The black scarf around her hips covered the rest of his hand with its fringes, and the hidden mystery of what he might do next shot a buzzing thrill through her.

When he rubbed, she reacted with a jerk. He smiled knowingly down at her.

Dangerous, she thought, grasping at a thread of common sense that unfurled through her brain. He was a near stranger who had way too much sway over her right now.

But she was allowing him to do this, so she could handle it. She *wanted* it, and she was ready to take what was being offered.

He was running his fingers across her leg, getting closer, then dragging away from the ache between her thighs.

"I've already had about fifteen fantasies about you in these boots," he whispered.

He almost sounded shy. Sure. As if this Romeo was capable of shy.

Still…he'd already had fantasies? About her?

"When I saw you in the bar," he continued, fingers reaching her outer thigh then, slowly, so slowly, traveling back inward, "it only took me about a second to invent a scenario."

Ooooh. His naked admission speared into her, turning her on like a solar flare.

His fingers strayed to her inner thigh, and she flinched again in reaction, hitching in a tight breath.

"Tell me," she said. "Just tell me what you imagined."

In the half-darkness, he smiled again—more to himself than anything else, she thought. He toyed with her nerve endings, drawing her out with every exploring touch.

"It's nothing too out there." He stroked upward. "I just wondered if you were going to let me—" he glided his thumb into the crevice between her legs "—do something like this."

When he pressed her clit, she strained against him, crying out softly. She didn't even have time to suck in another ounce of oxygen before he began massaging her. Even through her thin pants, his touch was electric.

In the midst of this, she had no shame. Why should she? Tam was a woman, one who craved and needed, one who knew right now *exactly* what she wanted and wasn't ashamed to claim it.

She echoed his strokes with tiny movements of her hips, encouraging him, showing them both that she was the kind of woman who went for what she wanted.

"I haven't," she said between pulsations, "worn these…boots at all…. This is…first time."

"Good." With every subtle thrust of his thumb, he watched her, as if entranced by the show. "I'm just going to go ahead and think that they're all mine, then."

At least for tonight, she thought. They didn't need to clarify that. Didn't have to make promises about the future when this was enough for now.

Beats of a building hunger slammed through her, faster, harder. He circled with more intensity, wedging his arm behind her head so it didn't knock against the wall with every push.

Then, kissing her again, he used his tongue to accentuate and echo the drives of his thumb, the gyrations of her hips.

She clung to him for life and sanity. And bit by bit the sharp anguish between her legs expanded, heated, grew until it ate away at every inch of her.

When she came, it was in tearing doses, one climax, two, wave upon wave of pounding release and quiet fury. She groaned into his neck with each blow until she was done.

For a second she couldn't move, could only hold on to his shoulders and slump against him, dizzy and weak. Part of her was afraid to look at him, to see if he was done with her. Part of her wanted to drink him in so she could assuage this thirst that'd hardly been slaked.

No guilt, she told herself. Don't you dare start thinking about divorce, rejection and all the times you've been dumped before. Just *live*.

As he ran a hand over her hair, she realized that maybe he didn't think it was as unattractive as she'd always assumed. For a moment she was able to at least let go of one hang-up.

Now she just had to work on a few more.

MURPHY WAS FASCINATED with her hair—the corkscrews and tangles. He wondered if the complexity signified the woman.

If her blue gaze indicated anything, he'd suspect so. There were silent levels of thoughts in her eyes that she hadn't voiced yet. And she wouldn't voice them. Why would she feel the need to get deep with the type of date they both understood this to be?

A pang consumed him. He almost wished she would be around long enough for him to talk with her. That, along with the physicality of connecting, would make the night just about perfect. Because if he was honest with himself, he would admit that he'd never really gotten to know a woman, inside and out.

Hell. Murphy wasn't about to sit here and force noble intentions on himself. Come on, quality discussion wasn't the reason he'd brought Tam to this dark corner, now, was it? Not even remotely. He'd wanted some action, and this was just the tip of it. If Murphy had his way, he'd connect with a lot more of her. His nether regions were just about screaming and clawing to make *them* happy, too. Pleasuring her had been a whim…and maybe even a way of offering her something in exchange for what he'd decided to take tonight.

Still worked up, he pressed his lips to her forehead, a prelude to more. She stirred against him, and his groin—already willing—seized in anticipation.

"Going strong, huh?" She laughed a little.

He drew his fingertips down her temples, her face, then bent to fix his mouth to the spot where her ear met her jawline. She shivered, then turned into his kiss.

"Mmm," she mumbled against his mouth. "You're going to have me here all night, aren't you?"

"Not a bad plan," he whispered, angling to brush his mouth against her skin—that smoky, flowery musk, the scent of a free-love soul. Ironic, because this woman probably would've gotten along with Kyle better than she did with Murphy in the long run—or short run, based on the conditions of this date.

But Murphy was the one who had her now.

"Then if I'm staying awhile…" She tugged at his shirt until he lifted his head and met her gaze. She looked fevered, cheeks flushed and eyes wide. "What do you have planned?"

This time when he grinned, he didn't even have to summon Kyle's wolfishness. "I was thinking—" he raised her hands over her head until she reclined against the wall with a surprised smile "—that I could pose you like a work of art and paint you with more kisses."

He should've cringed at that, because Murphy Sullivan didn't talk in cornball lines. At least, he never had before.

With delight making her eyes sparkle, Tam answered before he could backpedal. "A man with my own passions." She relaxed into her new position, sending him a sultry look. "You into art?"

Even a guy like Murphy, who more often than not had his head buried in the sand, knew how to answer this one. Cater to a woman's interests when you had her at your fingertips. "I've got a great appreciation for it."

She sighed, and he kissed the shallow dip at the base of her throat, making her press into him.

Her voice vibrated through his lips as she talked. "I saw some of the best museums in the world—the Louvre, the Prado… You would love them. Or have you been…?"

"Unfortunately, I haven't." Was she talking so much because she wanted more of a mental link along with the sex, too? Murphy hadn't expected that, not from a girl who'd accepted Kyle's dating guidelines so easily.

But he could really like a woman who talked about

art, one who had a streak of intellectual curiosity and knowledge. Even if the conversation—and sex—would just be limited to tonight.

He looked up, smoothed back some hair from her forehead. "And what were you doing way over at the Louvre?"

Her face lit with a smile, and it satisfied him deep down, beneath the flailing hormones that were rearing up again to take over.

"I went to Europe before I moved here. Eight months backpacking through ten countries." She gave a tiny moan as Murphy cupped one breast, mapping it with a thumb. "We were all English majors, a reunion of college friends." She shifted, becoming more distracted by the play of his thumb around her hardening nipple. "Art museums, castles… Um, anyway, the point of the trip for me was to finally decide what I'd do with my life. Not that it worked."

"You wanted to discover yourself." While palming the small yet firm breast, he used his other hand to pull her shirt out of her pants. Yeah, he liked the talking, but he was getting worked up here, too.

"I'm actually still in the process."

She was watching him, as if trying to read his next move. Her mood struck Murphy as suddenly vulnerable, and he paused, caught off guard.

This wasn't the woman he'd walked out of the first bar with. God, this was…what? More the type of traditional girl he would take to, say, a restaurant where they could talk over wine and good food. See an art movie with. Take to that party given by a fellow firm coworker on Sunday night where he would schmooze and play the part of a future attorney.

This line of thinking was lethal. Even if Murphy's life could accommodate real dates and girlfriends—hell, his last relationship had lasted only four casual months before she had gotten sick of being ignored and had left him in the dust—he couldn't pursue things with Tam Clarkson. Murphy had seen to that when he'd lied to her about who he was. Pretending to be his cousin wasn't something he could countenance for more than a night. Even if his motives had been forty-five percent pure, the other fifty-five percent—which consisted of the out-of-control desire to experience the carefree life of Kyle—would guarantee her anger. And rightly so.

Bottom line? This was *it*. No second chances.

But…the Kyle side of Murphy realized something. That party this weekend? It was a masquerade thrown by an acquaintance and his wife to show off their wealth. It was a safe zone where everyone would be wearing masks to hide who they were. Which meant that if he took a woman who needed to be kept in the dark about his true identity, no one would know who he was anyway unless he wanted them to. It would also mean that *she* would never need to be revealed to anyone at the party.

His heart rate was picking up speed at the thought of more deception. Dammit, it was turning him on.

He imagined pulling the wool over the eyes of all those so-called brainiacs he worked with at Doyle, Flynn and Sullivan, fooling them by doing the unexpected beneath their noses. *Nobody would know who he was.…*

But even more intriguing was the possibility of entertaining Tam, the art lover. The guy throwing the party had often bragged about a small collection of Degas paintings that'd been handed down from previous generations. Something made Murphy long for the smile Tam would wear if she could see them. Something also made him yearn for the success of the small moral crime he would commit by extending this charade and fooling those pompous legal eagles.

Bang, bang, went his pulse, sounding like gunshots he was dodging. The adventure of it all was ratcheting up his adrenaline, addicting him into thinking it could be done.

The most important thing was that Tam never know how Kyle had rejected her. All Murphy was doing was the opposite, right? He would be risking a lot to *be* with her, introducing her into a situation that would only make her happy.

When he saw that she was gauging him with a tilted head, probably wondering why he'd come to a cold stop while divesting her of her blouse, he resumed his Kyle smile.

He didn't want this to end tonight.

His heart rammed in his chest like the enemy breaking down an impossible door. Blood rushed to his groin, renewing the pulsing grind of hunger. He bent to kiss her, gathering her in his arms and seeking something he hadn't found anywhere else.

Somewhere a phone rang, toodling a Mozart tune.

At first, Murphy barely noticed, he was so lost in her. But when she hesitated, he found his way out of the kiss, his lips seared by the contact.

"You're *kidding* me." Tam bent down to grab her phone from the purse she'd dropped to the ground.

She made quick work of answering, talking and hanging up. "My friend Danica. She's on a date, too, but it wasn't going as smoothly as…well, *this*."

Was she blushing? Murphy was utterly charmed by that. And he was ready to get back to what the call had interrupted.

She held up a hand, regret weighing down her smile. "We promised to go home together if one of our dates blew spectacularly. Hers did. I've—" she rolled her eyes and tucked in her shirt "—I've really got to go. I'm so sorry about this, but she drove because these hills make me nervous."

It was ending?

He ran a gaze over her: the wild hair, the uncertain smile of apology. The boots.

He didn't think before he spoke. Or maybe he'd done too much thinking when he'd come up with an alternative to never seeing her again.

"Sunday, there's this party…" What the hell was he doing?

She perked up, posture straightening. He could tell she might've been wondering if this had been it, too. If she'd been a grope-and-go date. He liked the validation his invitation had obviously given her. Liked it too much.

And, besides, added the devious wolf in him, they would be going to a masquerade. Masks. Hidden identities.

Just one more time, he thought. *I need more.*

And then I'll let go.

THE REAL KYLE SULLIVAN hadn't gone home after being lambasted by his cousin back at the Chinese lounge.

Hell, no. Things like judgmental lectures and disappointed gazes didn't bother Kyle because Murphy was so unbeatably perfect anyway. The family golden boy. A title this younger guy couldn't live up to, so he'd stopped trying years ago.

Instead Kyle had sloughed off his cousin's comments and gone on to Plan B, which included women, beer, rock 'n' roll and listening to the only person who knew what was best for Kyle.

Himself.

He'd arrived at Shaw O'Grady's not long after leaving Murphy to buy Tamara Clarkson a consolation drink. And as soon as Kyle ambled into what was said to be the second-oldest saloon in San Francisco, he was enveloped by the bass-through-the-floorboards music of a local band and the pleased hellos from the regulars. Kyle liked to come here when he didn't have firm plans. Thomas O'Grady, the great-great-grandson of Shaw, was a buddy, and the California women here were, as always, beautiful.

Kyle sat at the bar, near a table of what seemed to be a party of Phi-Kappa-lookin'-for-some-action girls. Their shirts were tight and their smiles freely given. Especially to Kyle.

Thomas was manning the bar, and he knew exactly what Kyle wanted. The older man slid a mug of Guinness on tap to his customer. Under his bushy mustache, he was grinning.

"Where you been?" he yelled over the music. "I thought you'd died and gone to hell."

"Not a chance," Kyle yelled back. "The devil can't stand the competition."

"Well, it's awful nice of you to grace us with your presence. You know, I'm always expecting you to drag Murph in here with you, but—"

"But he's as ornery and bookish as ever." Kyle sipped his beverage. Smooth and dark. Soothing for the soul.

"Hey, hot guy!" It was a voice behind him—young and cocky and female, followed by the giggles of her friends.

He didn't turn around yet, and Thomas was amused by this. The bartender winked and left Kyle to engage the company of the sorority sisters when he was ready.

Why he wasn't ready, he didn't know. He just kept hearing Murphy's words over and over in his head: *What's so wrong with spending an hour with her? Just one goddamned hour?*

But what stung most was what Murphy hadn't said. It was more the way he'd looked at him: as though he'd been at the end of his rope with Kyle.

In truth, Murphy had given him plenty of those glances before, but this one had been different. Severely disheartened. It was that quality—the knowledge that maybe Murphy was hurting because he'd expected more of Kyle—that was eating away at him.

But, crap, he wasn't here to think about that. His cousin could jump into traffic as far as Kyle was concerned.

He took a bigger sip of beer, listened to the music, tapped his fingers on the bar.

Shallow. Dammit, that's what Murphy had said. *Shallow.*

Enraged, Kyle gulped down the rest of his beverage and gestured to Thomas for another.

"Hey!" the girl behind him said again.

Unwilling to deal with his conscience anymore, he glanced back at her. Bare-shouldered, tanned, blond, twentyish. She had the freshness of a waif who still slept with stuffed animals on her bed and wore panties that had "cutie" printed on the front of them. Suddenly Kyle felt very old.

But not mature. Murphy would've corrected him on that.

In a fit of rebellion, Kyle turned all the way around to face the girls. Screw his cousin. Kyle liked to have fun, unlike some people who preferred to hole up and labor their lives away. And guess what? After Murphy passed the bar, he'd be working eighteen hours a day for the rest of his life. Their cousin Ian sure did, and Murphy was too driven not to give the job his all, just like their older relative.

As the blonde crooked her finger at him, Kyle slid off his stool and walked on over.

Soon he was enclosed in a space of giggles and flirtation, and Kyle tried to like it.

He tried very hard.

5

THE NEXT COUPLE OF DAYS had gone by so slowly for Murphy that it'd felt like he was sitting in front of a stove watching water come to a boil. And it was all because of the urgency, fantasy and guilt that came with craving her.

He hadn't realized until now just how restless he was during the day at his cousin Ian's law firm as he continued doing grunt work, dotting the *i*s and crossing the *t*s in a dark-wooded room that choked him. And his nights had dragged, filled with bartending to pay off all his debts and dealing with Kyle, who hadn't talked to Murphy ever since The Big Scold outside of that Chinese lounge. Not that Murphy had any right to be so high and mighty. Every time he glanced at Kyle, he recalled his lies to Tam, remembered how wrong he'd been—even if it had felt right.

In the end, after the restaurant closed up shop and released him, he'd gone back to his place, where he'd stared at the research he brought home with him because he didn't know what else to do with himself.

Actually, that wasn't true. He knew exactly what he would rather be doing. And every bit of it had to do with the rush he'd felt while Tam had flirted with him, moaned against him.

He hated this animal side of himself just as much as he loved it, and as Sunday's masquerade party approached, he both dreaded and needed this next step in seeing just how much he could get away with. Friday night had triggered something deviant in him and, once found, he couldn't give it up.

Sure, it'd occurred to him that maybe, God, maybe he cared so little about what his professional contemporaries would think that it was worth the risk.

But in all honesty, he was more concerned about how Tam would react if he got caught—and he almost *welcomed* punishment because he knew he'd all too willingly jumped into a deception that he couldn't climb out of.

Still, that deception left him open to wondering if he could indeed wow her with the Degas paintings he knew she'd love, then sweep her away, have her all to himself, before any damage was done.

Riding on the mere thought of it, he'd chosen a dark costume with a cape, mask and hat to make sure no one called him "Murphy" in front of Tam tonight. And in order to show his host that he'd actually attended the party, Murphy had decided he would thank him personally tomorrow at the firm. That way, he could reveal details about the party to prove he'd been there, thus earning professional networking points, then apologize that he'd needed to leave so early.

The whole plan was ridiculous, warped—he could think of a thousand chiding words. Yet none of them was as powerful as the image of Tam's flushed cheeks as he'd made her come, the smile on her face when he'd invited her to the masquerade. He'd made her feel good, erased the sadness he'd seen earlier in the night when she'd been waiting for Kyle, and damned if that didn't supply him with enough excuses to continue.

This was how a daredevil must feel, he thought, standing on the edge of a cliff, ready to dive over it.

Sick bastard. He really *liked* it, too.

So, outside the gates of the Pacific Heights mansion where the orange glow from the windows cut through a slight fog, he waited, heart in his throat, for her to arrive. She'd elected to take a cab, refusing his offer of a ride even though this city was notorious for difficulty in securing taxis. But she'd insisted, ensuring that Murphy would stay at a distance: a fling who had no business seeing where she lived.

He couldn't blame her. Setting boundaries was a good idea, especially since this would be their last night together.

As a blur of headlights rounded the corner, his body clenched. His skin burned, eager to feel her again.

But when the car passed, he cursed, realizing just how far gone he was. His heart pounded like running footsteps, and he couldn't calm his excitement.

Why not go with the moment? asked a persuasive voice inside his head. *Stop fighting it. Let yourself go and don't worry.*

Pulse buzzing under his skin until it erased all doubts, Murphy leaned against the brick wall of the gate, slipping on his tricorn hat and mask.

Waiting for the woman he wanted more than anything.

IT WAS AROUND NINE O'CLOCK when Tam got out of the cab, clutching her half mask, and stepped onto the

sidewalk in front of the mansion. Live music—
something from the forties—winged over the thickened
air, exciting her senses.

She had a big thing for the exotic, romanticizing
every little detail. Maybe it was just because she was a
"dreamer"—just like her dad used to call her. She spent
a lot of time, especially in her Dillard Marketing
cubicle, doodling, looking through the want ads for her
dream job, planning but never quite completing.

But she was going to change all that. It'd started with
her moving here; it would continue when she finally
earned enough money to get out of her dad's house; and
it would go even further when she was finally secure
enough in her own life to start sharing it with someone
else.

In the future. Now she was content with the present.
Kyle.

Heartbeat spiking, she glanced around for him. Jeez,
was she a fool for meeting up again with a guy she'd
met in a bar? A guy she'd gotten to know on a superfi-
cial level and that was going to be it? It'd occurred to
her more than once that there was an awful chance she
was repeating history: putting her trust in someone who
would only work her over in the end.

As the cab pulled away into oblivion, she suddenly felt
very alone, even if Kyle was going to meet her any
minute.

What was she doing here?

Just roll with it, she thought. *You enjoyed being with
him the other night and you've been turned on for about
forty-eight consecutive hours because of it. Live for the
moment, okay?*

Okay. Yup. She could do this.

As someone stepped up behind her, she whirled around, the material of her costume swishing around her like a cloud.

"It's just me," said a male voice.

Kyle? Her belly warmed as a gush of yearning filled her.

He stepped in front of her, and she backed away because all she could see of him were his eyes through the mask. The *Amadeus*-style hat plus the mask, hid all identity. Add to that a long black cape over a tux and she wasn't sure if this was Kyle or someone she didn't know.

Then he swept off his hat and mask, revealing a face that caused the blood in her veins to stutter. He made her weak and so glad that she'd taken a chance on this invitation.

"Were you here the whole time?" she asked.

"Just a few feet away."

A slant of light caught his eyes, and without him having to say it, she knew he'd been watching her before revealing his presence. The hazy longing in his gaze told her that she had so much power over him that it robbed her of oxygen.

Her? Tamara Clarkson? She could affect a man like this?

She ignored the questions, knowing they were just covers for much more disturbing misgivings, and she didn't want to go there tonight.

He took a step closer, scanning the black veil she'd wound through and over her upswept hair; the dark of it covered her curls and added the required anonymity he'd emphasized after inviting her. Then he continued slowly looking her over, sliding his admiring gaze lower.

Stunned joy overtook her. Usually people looked at her unique clothes first, moved on to the friendly personality next and then maybe the rest of the package.

But not tonight. He'd been watching her face first, and he'd looked happy to see it, too.

She took a moment to revel in his attention while he appreciated all the effort she'd put into her costume. At work on Thursday, she'd started drawing plans for her creation, then abandoned them, as was her usual pattern. But the minute she'd gotten home, she'd visited her second bedroom where she stored mountains of material, then completed a fantasy: a swath of wispy gray here, a stream of filmy white there, a streak of sheer black. Because her body had still been thrumming from her orgasm, no doubt, she had been a little more confident than usual: she'd cut the long dress to flash some skin, to hint at what was below the costume.

But it didn't announce as much as suggest.

She held her breath as his gaze eased back upward, over her waist, her chest, her throat, her face.

"You're amazing," he said.

Tam almost dropped her mask. He didn't sound as if he was putting on the charm—not like the other night. No, he sounded as though he was somehow floored, just as out of breath as she was. It was a turnabout that surprised and pleased her.

His sincerity even drew her a little closer, made her wonder about everything she didn't know about Kyle Sullivan, how many sides he had.

"Thanks," she said. "I'm 'smoke.'" She held up her mask to show him its black simplicity, the sheer strips of material she'd attached to make it as ethereal as the fog hushing around them. "Smoke signals. Smoky glances. Smoke and mirrors."

"Clever."

"What are you?"

He laughed, carelessly gestured to his tuxedo and cape. But there was something dark passing over his eyes.

"What am I?" A slight smile tilted his lips. "I am my own dark side."

Headlights from an approaching car wiped over him. She caught a pulse-twisting glimpse of his smoothly shaven face, the angle of his cheekbones, the line of his jaw, the lips that tightened his smile ever so slightly....

Lips.

Bowled over, she could only think about what she'd give to have his mouth on hers again.

The tempo of her heartbeat slammed through her head, her chest, her sex. She felt the driving need to touch herself, to encourage her body.

To proceed with caution.

He must have noticed her hesitation. With persuasive gentleness, he reached out for her mask, lifted it to her face.

"See...we can be anyone we want to be tonight, Tam."

Wanting to believe it, she allowed him to help fix her mask in place. Maybe it was her imagination, but when he arranged her curls and veil so they hid the tied black band, she thought his touch was gentler than it'd been the other night.

But that wasn't likely. They both knew why they'd met up again, and it wasn't about building a solid relationship.

"Damn, I should've…" he said, shaking his head. But then he suddenly put on that killer grin and ran a finger below her chin. "Wait here for a sec."

Now this was more like it. No raw tenderness. Just living for the moment. This was the Kyle she'd made out with.

He walked to the gate opening fifty feet away, where a guard was posted in a tiny station, checking invitations, then came back. Odd. Why hadn't he taken her with him?

"Ready?"

He held his bent arm out to her, and she latched on to it, not bothering with petty questions.

Tonight was about one thing.

And that didn't include nagging at the guy who was about to show her the way to her dreams.

THEY COULD BE ANYONE they wanted to be tonight.

Murphy kept that in mind as he and Tam wandered the nineteenth-century mansion with drink in hand. He wasn't imbibing—his mask, which he didn't dare take off, wouldn't allow his mouth access to the glass—but that was fine. Just so Tam was having a good time, he was content.

They'd kept their conversation light, nothing out of the ordinary. He'd also done a damned good job of steering her away from anyone he knew. Every time there was a close call, his body revved in a way that he realized he shouldn't be enjoying.

But he was. God, he was.

He loved seeing an old partner from the firm squint-

ing at him, trying to ferret out his identity. And when
the associate who'd invited him had headed in their direction for some obvious conversation, he'd thought it
was over. But by some trick of fate, his acquaintance
had been intercepted by a drunken cohort, and the resulting high had energized Murphy. Too bad his cousin
and boss, Ian, wasn't a partygoer, because that might've
been the biggest challenge of all.

They'd finally come upon the library, where he knew
the two Degas paintings were kept behind protective
glass display cases. Around them, walls of books lan-
guished under the dim glow of art-friendly lighting.
He'd been keeping tabs on the area to see when the
room might be empty and had pounced when he thought
the coast was clear.

His pulse thumped as they went to the center of the
room, and he realized that he was more excited about
the look he would see on Tam's face than anything else.

When she saw the painted dancers, shaded in blue
and graced with beauty, she held a hand to her throat.
When she spoke, her voice was choked with an emotion
so startling, he couldn't define it.

"Oh, my God, Kyle. Did you know they were here?"

He felt his skin heating under the mask, and it wasn't
necessarily because of lust or the daredevil anticipation
of being discovered. He thought he might be blushing
because he'd affected her on such an obviously
profound level.

"I knew." He walked over to a desk, where he could
recline and watch the play of emotion on her lips. "I
invited you because of them."

And a few more reasons he wouldn't go into.

She didn't say anything for a while, just slowly ambled closer, as if the work would disappear if she moved too quickly. She set down her wine on a stone coaster that waited on a nearby table, never taking her eyes off the art as security cameras tracked her.

He had enough respect to keep to himself. Besides, watching her was doing something to him. He couldn't take his gaze away.

Something so simple, he thought. It'd been so damned easy to make her glow again.

His chest warmed, but he tamped down the pleasure, knowing it was out of order.

He didn't know how much time passed. But when he heard the shuffle of people in the hall, he realized his number was up.

"Tam?" God, he hated to bring her out of this.

She turned around, a dreamy grin on her face. It made him want to take her to a thousand exhibits.

"Thank you," she said, coming over to him and clasping his hands.

She was so close he could've kissed her, so close that his lips tingled with the possibility. A feather's breadth away…

Drunken voices jarred their gazes apart, and Murphy pointed toward a second exit on the other side of the room.

"I'm not in the mood for anyone else," he said, wrapping an arm around her waist and guiding her away. They made it out a mere second before the others entered.

They found themselves in another empty hallway, flames flickering in wall lanterns and casting a bourbon-soft hue. More security cameras whizzed, craning to see them. To their right, French doors led to a garden outside. He angled her toward them, hoping there'd be no cameras outdoors.

"I can't believe you didn't tell me about the paintings!" Tam said.

"It was a little surprise."

"This is really great, Kyle. Not only the art, which just blew me away, but...jeez, wandering around in costume in an old house. It definitely makes me feel...different."

"How so?"

"Like..."

They came to the doors, and he reached to open them, glancing down at her at the same time. When he saw the expression on her face—a look of utter desire and gratefulness aimed right at him—the air seemed to suck out of the hallway.

"Like a proper girl who's meeting some illicit lover," she continued in a soft voice. "A Barbary Coast outlaw who waits outside for her until every light in the house has been extinguished." She slid a finger into his collar, touching his skin and just about lighting it on fire. "Is that why you brought me here, Kyle? To get my fantasies in motion?"

Overcome, he grasped her waist, rubbing his thumbs against the sheer material. It rasped with every stroke.

Her breathing was coming quicker, her eyes going unfocused.

Without another word, she acted before he did, opening the doors, taking him outside to the massive backyard. The farther they got from the main house, the more the music was taken over by the hush of night, the lace of sifting fog, the splash of fountains among trails of garden and flowers.

"As an outlaw, you'd hide in the darkest place while you waited," Tam said after she'd found a fountain in a far corner with an angel looking up to the sky, wings spread.

She gently pushed Murphy to a seat on the wide, circular fountain bench, where she stood above him. They were completely alone out here, and his body was taking itself to the next level of stimulation—from the wallop of getting away with being at the party without anyone knowing, to the anticipation that had been building all night to touch Tam.

Tam reached for his mask, clearly intending to remove it. He jerked back, then surreptitiously looked around for cameras. The mask had been his savior all night; losing it had been unthinkable.

But there were no security devices anywhere.

"Dammit, Kyle, it's driving me nuts. I want to see you now that we're outside and the masquerade is inside."

Slowly he pulled off the hat and the mask. As crisp air misted over his skin, the full view of Tam welcomed him. In the moonlight, her veil looked like a dark halo.

"There." She dropped his mask on the bench next to him, then touched his face. "I can see you now."

Remorse skimmed him, leaving mental abrasions. She couldn't see *him*. She hadn't removed the invisible mask he wore.

Without thinking, he reached up to her, dragged her down, kissed her softly. In apology. In pure desire.

He tried not to dwell on what his family or his friends, damn, on what *Tam* would think of him if they

knew everything. Worst of all, he could barely stand to
face his own judgment. So he lost himself in her: the
taste of her need for him, the acceptance of what she
thought he was offering her.

Their lips moved in seductive cadence, slick,
starving nips and strokes of tongue. His hands smoothed
over her back and hips in a desperate quest for her...for
something he couldn't grasp.

She came up for air, leaning her forehead against his.
But her hands stayed busy, parting his cape and coasting
down his chest and lower, near the fly of his pants.

Murphy's belly spasmed under her fingertips.

"A woman of experience," he managed to say. "I
thought you were some innocent in that fantasy of
yours."

"Innocent," she said. "Is that what you like, Kyle?"

"I like it any way it comes, with you." He gasped as
her fingers dipped into his waistband.

She toyed with him, running teasing fingers back and
forth against his skin. She was killing him.

At his limit, he shifted her around, laying her on the
wide bench, her veil pooled behind her head.

She made a pleased sound, halfway between a sigh
and a laugh. "See, I think you actually like someone
who's got some sexual mileage, Kyle. Someone who
can keep up with you."

"And you did just fine the other night."

This time she did laugh, and he savored it.

"Tell me," she said. "Where's the wildest place
you've ever had sex?"

She was only keeping it light and easy, as per her
agreement with Kyle. It didn't take him long to come

up with an answer, either. He'd had more than a few casual girlfriends in the past; some of them liked to push the boundaries of the bedroom more than others, and he'd been only too glad to oblige.

"I guess," he said, tracing a palm over Tam's stomach, "the wildest place would be in the corner of a French Quarter bar. The room was so crowded that nobody was paying attention, and the table blocked most of what we were doing while she sat on my lap and hiked up her short skirt and—"

"Whoa." Tam had lifted her head to shoot a wide-eyed gaze at him. Even underneath her half mask, he could tell she was enticed. "That's brave."

Now that he thought about it, he'd gotten off on the danger of that encounter, just as he was now. He should've noticed his bent back then, taken better care to deal with it.

Wanting to subdue all analytical thought, Murphy started to slide his hand upward, toward Tam's breast. But, tease that she was, she laughed again and turned over so she was facing away, a taunt that lured him.

"Now I'll tell you about *my* wildest place," she said.

6

TAM KNEW WHAT her comments were doing to him: his intent gaze, his taut body and the set of his mouth had all let on that he was getting pushed closer and closer to the edge.

She wanted to spin that out, torture him a little. The control she obviously had over him—a first for her—stoked her to the boiling point. Teasing him felt like the right thing to do with a been-there, done-that man like Kyle who expected her to be just as practiced as he was. She was betting that plain vanilla sex wasn't going to do it for him, that he would respond to her games more than the drab truth: that Tam, herself, wasn't much experienced beyond conventional sex.

It shocked her to realize that she'd never been properly seduced before, the foreplay of previous encounters just a formality before the actual act. Kyle was showing her what she'd missed: sweet tension, coiled anticipation, leading up to a final, incredible and inevitable release.

The gurgle of the fountain tickled her ears as she got comfortable lying flat on her stomach. She didn't want him to see her face as she created what he no doubt wanted to hear. Her expressions of inexperience would be a dead giveaway.

He sketched over her spine, exploring the curve of her back. Tam shivered, feeling her nipples bead.

Her voice shook a little. "Back when I was on that European trip, we stopped in Florence, Italy."

"Right. Your big trip overseas."

She'd mentioned it to him the other night and, suddenly, she realized that she talked about it a lot. That was because it was really the only life experience she had.

She ignored the emptiness of that and went back to being flirty. She'd become an expert at internalizing since that night she'd heard her parents argue. A master at pretending everything was hunky-dory, she squeezed her innermost thoughts beneath her skin where they wouldn't show, even though they could still be felt.

As she stirred underneath Kyle's hand, she said, "You know what they say about those Italian men, right?"

He laughed, his fingers moving lower, stroking one cheek of her rear end. The mock silk and gauze of her dress sighed against her.

Her sex began to prime itself, swelling into dampness. The air was sharp and shallow in her lungs. "At a club, I managed to meet a guy who was angry at his girlfriend, not that I knew it at the time. So he took me to what I thought was a random building nearby, and we settled in just outside an open window—"

She choked to a halt. He'd pushed up her dress, and cool air brushed over her legs. But they were warmed by his hand as he skimmed it up the flesh of her calves, higher, higher...

"And?" he asked softly.

The material slumped back down as he continued

upward, slipping his fingers between her knees and pausing there, tickling her inner thighs.

She swallowed hard, her clit pounding. In the background of the fountain's splash, the music played on, reminding her that someone could discover them at any moment.

She licked her lips, mouth dry. "I found out that he'd positioned us right below his girlfriend's window, where she could…hear us…."

Kyle had shifted, gliding his other hand under her dress. Now he was working her panties off and down her legs.

In the near distance, someone laughed in the night.

Tam's sex seemed to lurch, juices trickling down her inner thighs.

"Then?" Kyle asked, voice ragged.

Her heart was fluttering against her breastbone. Way too conscious of the approaching voices, she started to turn over.

"Someone's coming." She sounded almost frantic to her own ears, but was it because she was afraid or excited?

"And I hope it'll be you," Kyle said.

He managed in one smooth maneuver to ease her to her back, push up her dress and coax open her legs, exposed, vulnerable. The night air laved her. She pounded with the expectation of being touched and satisfied.

With a grin, he paused above her. His eyes had gone dark, nearly feral, relaying once again how much power she had over him. That she *owned* him. It was a heady second, making her feel like the sexiest woman ever to walk the world.

And she wanted to be that woman, wanted him to crave her more than water or food or any other female who'd ever given him pleasure. In this moment, she knew she could do it, too.

But deep down, something still niggled at her.

She owned him, all right. But only in body.

As she looked into his eyes, it didn't seem to be enough. Yet it would have to be.

With maddening slowness, he drew his gaze to the most intimate part of her, opened and waiting and beating.

"So did the girlfriend catch you two outside her window?" Kyle asked.

Without waiting for an answer, he lowered himself under the screen of her dress, kissed a bare inner thigh, drank a stream of wetness from her skin.

Tam's body clamped into itself, her clit burning. She groaned and her mind wheeled, but she still choked out an answer. "Yeah, she…"

Closer, Kyle was getting closer…

The air grated out of her as he hit the target and pushed open her knees, his tongue licking upward, parting her.

Oh…good…he was so *good* at this.

She cradled his head and moved with his erotic kisses, her brain blanking out, her body mounting and mounting with pressure.

Nibbling, exploring, he sucked on her. The laughter and conversation of the wandering couple in the background became more distinct as the party's music stopped. Grasping for something, anything, her hand reached into the fountain, touching only liquid.

He panted, rested his cheek against her thigh. "The party can't be over."

"Just…starting." Tam's voice was hushed, panicked.

With a soft laugh, he went back to kissing her center.

Spreading her with his fingers, he circled her clit with his tongue, tasting the musky sweetness of the stiffened nub.

She gave a little cry, and Murphy groaned against her, his cock hard and screaming for relief.

As Tam grew more agitated beneath his mouth, he put all his energy into bringing her to an arching surrender, using his fingers and tongue and lips, working her by nipping and sucking. He was about to explode, the rush of blood to his erection driving him.

She squirmed beneath him, made tiny sounds that elevated and mingled with the fountain drops. Then, with a muffled shriek, she grabbed his hair and flooded his mouth with a climax so violent that it tore into him, too.

Beyond thinking, Murphy gave in to himself—to *her*—and pulled her onto his lap. She ended up straddling him, legs bent as she pressed against him with such intensity he thought he would lose it. As his hard-on settled between her thighs, it pulsed, as if his heartbeat was trying to push into her.

"Kyle," she said, as if she were hurting.

That name. His devil-may-care persona. The man he wanted to be, at least for tonight. The unleashed side of himself that needed to feel her slick muscles clenching around his dick and drawing him deeper and deeper into her.

Lost in a vortex, he tore at his fly.

"Condom." Tam pushed aside his cape and started to search for his wallet.

But he beat her to it, stripping it out and tossing it to

the ground. Together, in the midst of temple-pounding abandonment, they both managed to sheath him.

Kyle. That's who she wanted. And she would get him.

Urgently he took her by the hips and drove into her, sucking in a sharp breath at the feel of being buried and surrounded. Perfect.

He worked her over his cock, grinding into her as her dress crinkled around them. Adjusting to the rhythm, she used her legs to capture him deeper, up and down, up and down, like butterfly wings.

Guiding her, he pressed her pelvis closer, harder, increasing the speed and force of every churn.

The night seemed to have gone thickly silent, cut only by his building pulse and her ecstatic whimpers.

Up, down, up, down…

It seemed to last for hours, days. When she leaned her head back and moaned, he stepped it up, moving her hips faster, faster…

As she stiffened, fisting his cape, her voice stretched into a long cry that seemed to pierce him, traveling to his chest, his arms, his legs, his cock—

Like a resurrected creature crashing out of the ground, he burst. *Tam,* he thought, her name falling through his mind, through his body like sparks from a fireworks explosion. *Tam.*

They clung to each other, her body slumped against him. He buried his face in the upswept ribbons and curls of her hair, taking in her earthy scent.

He'd never felt so liberated, his lungs crisp with night air, his body coursing with residual adrenaline.

And he'd never felt so trapped in himself.

For a few moments he lulled her with his hands underneath her dress: on her thighs, her calves. Stroked her until he convinced himself that this was all still harmless.

Now there were voices just on the other side of the hedge that hid the fountain, so he adjusted the material around her.

She drew back and, under the half mask she still wore, watched him with bright eyes. "Party crashers," she panted, referring to the company that could round the hedge at any second. Her face was pink, dewed with sweat.

He ignored all the wired emotions flapping around inside his chest. "Wouldn't they have gotten an eyeful?"

Adrenaline cooling, he made sure she was pieced back together, because he could still hear the nearby chatting and, though he was enjoying pushing the envelope, he wouldn't subject Tam to the certain awkwardness of *flagrante delicto*.

A perverse thought entered his mind. Did the real Kyle take the time to be as attentive after sex as Murphy was being now?

Cut it out, he thought as he took off the condom and zipped back up. It felt right to be Murphy in this respect. But, even so, he didn't stop himself from falling back into the playboy attitude that Tam seemed to want from him. It was getting to be a too-comfortable fit.

"So…" Looking away from him, she busied herself by putting her panties back on. "Is there a post party somewhere?"

His first instinct was to gather her up and take her home with him, where they could be alone. But then he saw a glint of hope—and another emotion?—creeping into her gaze.

No. This wasn't how it was supposed to go. A girl who'd assured Kyle that she only wanted fun wasn't supposed to request something genuine. Things had already progressed past the single-night fling he'd initially limited himself to. And Murphy had gone way beyond that one drink he'd promised to give her to make up for Kyle's rejection.

But now, seeing as how Murphy had screwed up so royally, didn't he owe her more than just orgasms for his deception? How the hell could he bring her home and take further advantage when he'd already taken too much?

"Work," he said softly, putting an end to this before he could change his mind. "Tomorrow I've got to go to work—" He almost added something about Doyle, Flynn and Sullivan but caught himself. The reminder of his lies only fanned the self-disgust that was starting to burn.

"Oh." Tam focused on tidying her dress. "You're right. Monday's a work day. Forgot about that."

"Tam…"

"Don't start apologizing." She put on a cheery smile and shrugged. "We both went into this knowing it was just a thing. No commitments or worries, okay?"

He desperately wanted to buy into that, but couldn't. Her smile seemed too spunky, and her veil was askew. It was almost as if he was seeing the woman who'd won his sympathy in that Chinese lounge while waiting for the blind date who'd ditched her. It drove a blade of guilt through his chest.

And it also reminded him of how stranded he would feel without this charade.

He wasn't ready to give up Kyle's life, give *Tam* up,

if he was totally honest. Yet he had to. Had no choice if he wanted to look at himself in the mirror and not despise the sight of this stranger who'd emerged.

Tam got to her feet before he did. When she began walking away without him, he knew the extent of her hurt, even if she was hiding it underneath that smile.

Nice going, he thought to himself. *And you thought Kyle was an asshole.*

Remembering all too well that he needed to put on his mask, he entered the mansion behind her and discreetly disposed of the condom in a covered wastebasket in an empty bathroom. Only a few stragglers remained, and as the few people stared at this unknown man and woman who'd ghosted through the party, Murphy knew that he was making the right choice by cutting loose. He could've been caught tonight and created a world of trouble for himself and Tam.

He couldn't deny that he'd enjoyed tempting fate by showing up with her, by deceiving everyone. But he'd lost his taste for deceiving Tam.

"So DID YOU GET CAUGHT?"

It was lunchtime on Monday in the lounge of the Wentworth-Holt Building, where the Sisters of the Booty Call were meeting once again. The last to share her story, Tam had just related most of her dating adventures with Kyle to everyone, toning much of it down for public consumption, of course.

As Julia Nguyen waited for an answer to her question, Danica mixed the business cards in The Boot. She and Tam had already caught up with each other, first during their carpool home Friday night, then during a phone call Sunday after Tam had gotten home from the party. Danica had also been the first Sister to tell everyone about her own Friday-night story. Dana the attorney sucked, he was arrogant and way too conservative. She couldn't draw another card soon enough, yadadee, yadadoo.

But Tam had kept it casual in her conversations with her friend, being careful not to show how disappointed she was that she would never get to see Kyle again.

If she'd read him right.

After he'd begged off because of work the next day—oldest excuse in the book—they'd left the party. But the great sex had obsessed her, making her crave more. And why not? Two orgasms. Two. It was hard enough to get one going, but…phew. *Two.*

So, like a junkie, Tam had asked him to drop her off at her place in his Jeep. Yes, she'd finally revealed where she lived to him. It'd been a subtle hint—jeez, a next *step*— that should've screamed that she was offering another personal detail. That she wouldn't mind another date.

Mind? Heck, she'd kill to get it on with Kyle again.

But he'd driven away, leaving her to stare at the ceiling most of the night, wondering what would be the harm in keeping a good thing going while it lasted.

Now, in the Sisters' lounge, Tam cleared her throat and went into PG-13 mode as she answered Julia. "No, we didn't get caught, so don't get excited. It sounded like that laughing couple sat down somewhere on the other side of the fountain hedge so they never made it over to our make-out spot."

Make-out. That was a euphemism if Tam had ever heard one.

Her body went elastic just thinking about what he'd done to her: his lips and tongue so skillful, his erection so deep inside her she'd—

"What're the chances for another date?"

That was Pamela Hoff, with her platinum ringlets gathered in a ponytail. She was reigning at her normal position, leaning against the lounge wall.

Teena of the brown spiky hair jumped in, too. Today, to confirm a clear shoe fetish, she was wearing strappy fiesta-colored flats and a suit to match. "Chances sound pretty positive from what you told us."

"I don't know," Tam said, playing it down. "This wasn't meant to be a search for the love of my life or anything."

"She's just tasting all the chocolates in the box before choosing a favorite," added Danica. "Kind of like her temp job, you know? Sample before settling."

Even though the reminder got to Tam, the philosophy did make her feel better about maybe never going out with Kyle again. Dating was a process of elimination, and it was meant to be enjoyable. Free spirits didn't weigh themselves down.

Heck, Tam knew that she was only reacting to the physical sensations Kyle had aroused. If he didn't call again, she could find hot lovin' elsewhere.

Even if she did feel at the top of her spirits when he looked at her.

"I don't know, Danica," Milla Page said. The Internet expert watched Tam from the sofa. "Our girl looks like she's picked out a truffle that's definitely got her sweet tooth."

There was a reflective hesitation from the occupants

of the lounge at large. Tam put on a mask of indifference, diverting them from what she was really feeling.

Mercedes Estevez had been quietly showing two other women a new spa cream, but she glanced up as she also considered the newest Sister. "There's just something about you today, Tamara. A difference from last week."

"That's because she's ready to take Kyle Sullivan *on*," Danica said.

Tam met her friend's assessing gaze, noticing something in its depths. A glimmer of hope that at least someone in this room would find the right man?

"I'm just glad you guys got me to participate," Tam said, forcing some breeziness. "Last week was just what I needed."

"Good!" Julia Nguyen checked her watch to keep the meeting well-paced, then looked around the room. "Any other stories?"

"Ribald tales?" added Teena, jokingly wringing her hands together like a letch.

Pamela laughed. "Julia, not all of us can boast about yet *another* date with our Boot men."

The Vietnamese woman smiled, obviously pleased with the progress of her own love life.

Gaze still hopeful, Danica held out The Boot to Tam, testing her with the chance to draw someone else's name. To embark on another opportunity just in case Kyle had gotten his fill of her.

"Nah," Tam said, going on a whim. "I'll take a week off."

Danica held it there a second longer. "You sure?"

"Absolutely." She needed a rest, right? It's not like

she was sitting this round out for Kyle. If he didn't call, so what? She wouldn't dial him up, either. In fact, she could take this week to think about whether or not she wanted to give The Boot another shot.

With an understanding smile, Danica plucked out a card, putting her own single self back into the mix.

Back into the dating pool where, at any time, they could all drown.

THAT NIGHT, after Amidala had closed its doors to all customers, and the restaurant staff was cleaning up, Kyle clocked out and then hung around the manager—to see how a restaurant ran as much as to shoot the crap, really. After a while he wandered over to the bar, where Murphy was grinning to himself and deftly polishing glasses, then putting them away.

They hadn't talked for nearly a week, now—only when they had to during work hours or when they'd used chopped phrases during Sunday brunch at the folks'. Kyle told himself he didn't care much about the lack of Murphy in his life. Who needed a stone Buddha sitting on your chest? His cousin was a drag. No loss.

The only reason he was coming within shouting distance right now was that Aunt Bridget had asked him to remind Murphy about getting his cousin Ian to brunch this weekend since they hadn't seen him in a month.

Aunt Bridget didn't enjoy phone conversation. If a message could be relayed through the grapevine of family members, that was more than good enough. She trusted her boys to do her bidding, too, and they were damned sure smart enough not to let her down.

Kyle came nearer, grabbed a hand towel and picked up a glass, imitating Murphy's motions. When he caught himself, he made an effort to speed up and differentiate his movements from his cousin's.

Murphy must've noticed Kyle's deliberate attempts to work his own way, too, because a bigger smile quirked over his mouth. Even though he didn't say anything, it still burned Kyle that he'd caught on.

"Your ma wants me to remind you about getting Ian—"

"I already know," Murphy said, effortlessly dispatching the glasses.

Then again, everything Murphy did was effortless. He never messed up at whatever he tried.

Kyle tried not to let that get to him, but it already had—years and years ago when he'd first realized that Murphy was the wonderful one and he was the family joke.

"If you already know," Kyle said, "why did she tell me to tell you?"

Murphy shot him a pointed look, and Kyle realized that he'd been had by Aunt Bridget. Crap, the woman had taken him and his sisters in when they were grass-high, and he still didn't know when she'd maneuvered him to her purposes.

"She's concerned about our recent lack of communication." With slick grace, Murphy twirled a glass and set it in place.

"Is she now?" Kyle tried Murphy's glass trick and almost dropped it.

Luckily Murphy didn't see. Or maybe he had, but he just didn't say anything.

They didn't talk—not about cousin Ian and especially not about last Friday. Addressing each other while avoiding the bigger subject had always been their way of making amends; they'd grown up together and could read each other that well. And from the way Murphy hadn't gotten all stiff when Kyle approached, he could tell that things had improved between them.

But Kyle knew that Murphy hadn't changed his mind about the shallowness part. It wouldn't be that easy.

Murphy had settled back into that absent grin Kyle had walked in on. Uh-huh, a grin. What was wrong here?

Kyle made a show of glancing under the bar and then at his cousin.

"What?" Murphy tossed his towel to the side where it landed squarely on a pile of rags that would be taken to the back. Neat trick.

Kyle shrugged. "Nothing."

Now Murphy checked below the bar.

Kyle grinned, liking that his cousin had fallen for the bait. "Just wondering if there was some bar bunny underneath that wood putting a smile on you."

"Smile?" Murphy grew serious. "I wasn't smiling."

"No, not at all. That sort of thing takes away from work time."

Whisking his fingers over his mouth, Murphy seemed to think about this. Then, miracle of miracles, he smiled again.

"See," Kyle said. "No smiles around here."

"Just happy to get off duty."

When Murphy met his eyes, Kyle was shocked to see something even more out of the ordinary: his cousin's gaze wasn't distracted or at all businesslike. There was something else there, something almost…

"What gives?" Kyle asked.

Murphy started to shrug, then stopped. He furrowed his forehead. "I'm just… Never mind."

Suddenly it hit him. "You thinking about a girl?" He angled another glance at his cousin. "I know that look— it's standard issue for guys."

Astoundingly, Murphy didn't deny. He didn't confirm, either. "Drop it, Kyle."

He was about to say something like, "Then go out there and get it while it's hot," but he remembered last Friday and how that sort of sentiment had gotten him into Murphy's bad graces.

And maybe Kyle *had* been kind of callous with that girl from the business card setup. What was her…? He couldn't remember her name. But he would think about it. Forgetting her name gnawed at him because it was proof of what Murphy had said.

So Kyle did drop it. Kind of.

"All I have to say is that you need to grab hold of whatever's making you grin." Because the more Murphy grinned, the happier he'd be, and it'd be that much easier to gain forgiveness from him.

Not that Kyle would admit it, but he liked to have Murphy on his side. His cousin's disappointment stung too much.

His words seemed to shake Murphy up, because his cousin just stared at him for a moment. There was something like confusion in the other man's stance, and that shocked Kyle.

Had he actually said something that was worthwhile?

Content with the possibility, Kyle tossed his towel to the side, just as Murphy had done. The cloth landed smack-dab where it needed to be.

Then he walked away, unable to help his own grin from emerging.

7

YOU NEED TO GRAB HOLD of whatever's making you grin,
Kyle had said. And Murphy had actually listened to his
well-meaning cousin.

Probably not a good thing to use Kyle as a guidance
counselor but, God love him, he'd said exactly what
Murphy had wanted to hear, and Murphy had seized
the advice.

Now, as Murphy sat in his covered Jeep in front of
Tam's stately home that same night, he decided it'd
actually been more like what his libido had wanted to
hear.

Not that all this beating himself up mattered anyway,
because this would be the very last time he'd see her.

Really. None of this would matter after tonight.

Through his windshield he could see dark clouds
gathering in the post-midnight sky. They were heavy
with a rain that was bound to fall. A mixture of sulfur
and moisture encompassed the pricey Victorians and
mansions.

At least, they might as well have been mansions, in
Murphy's eyes. He was used to more modest dwellings
in his neck of the town.

He inhaled, then blew out a breath as he exited the

car. When he'd phoned from his cell—he'd encouraged her to use that number instead of Kyle's work phone since he had "a new boss who doesn't like personal calls"—Tam had sounded happy to hear from him, even as he apologized for calling so late.

There'd been no talking around the subject of why he'd gotten in touch. Knowingly, she'd told him to drop by tonight, and he'd agreed, counting the minutes until he arrived.

One more visit, he repeated to himself, just to get this crazy obsession out of his system and tell her a decent goodbye. She deserved that, right? At the very least.

Grasping the expensive bottle of Petite Syrah he'd splurged on from his tips, Murphy approached her father's home, stray raindrops pelting him like tiny stones.

The building was impressive. Under a glow of artificial lighting, the facade was pale yellow, topped by rust-hued roofing. With its two stories, slim chimney and large square windows, it reminded Murphy of a gingerbread house without the icing. Aesthetically stark, it ruled the view from the top of a hill that overlooked the Bay Bridge.

He couldn't imagine her in this place. Like a lot of things about Tam Clarkson, the pieces didn't quite fit together. An earthy woman who lived in a wealthy home. A big talker who seemed to carry an edge of innocence.

He was fascinated, in spite of himself.

Circling to the back of the house, Murphy ducked a few more raindrops. She'd told him that she would wait on her bedroom balcony while she had a glass of wine.

As he glanced up, he saw her, bundled in blankets on a lawn chair.

"Tam?"

She didn't respond. Had he taken so long to arrive that she'd given up on him and fallen asleep?

The thought of seeing Tam with her eyes closed and her cheeks flushed with slumber got to Murphy. Instead of yelling at her to wake up, he set down the wine on the grass, then took a running leap at some iron grating that wound up the house to the balcony.

It was an easy trip. As he finished his climb, he saw that she was indeed getting her fill of shut-eye. He paused, drinking her in under the dim balcony lighting, grinning because she looked so damned sweet. Her hair was all tumbled, her lips parted, her skin pinkened and dewed with the beginning of the rain.

Something started to zing around his chest, outlining the area of his heart.

Oh, great. Here he was, getting the damned tingles for a girl he couldn't possibly pursue. Perfect.

Still, he moved closer, coming to a crouch by her chair. Holding his breath, he touched his fingertips to her cheek.

The sky grumbled and more raindrops began shimmering down.

Closing his eyes, he leaned nearer, smelling her fresh skin, then kissed her once on the temple, tasting rain and warmth.

Damn, he wanted to take all of her into him, consume her as much as she consumed him.

He kissed her again, on the mouth, this time. "Tam?" he whispered against her.

"Mmm." She opened her lips, then slowly sipped at him, as if she were in the middle of a dream and he'd stumbled into the best part of it.

Jarred by the purity of the moment, he buried a hand in her hair and languidly kissed her. The pace reminded him of stirring thick honey, and that's even how she tasted—sweet and rich with all the things he would never get to discover about her. Things that were beginning to tug at him, to interest him more than was healthy.

The clouds loosened, releasing a light, steady patter. Automatically Murphy broke away to shield her dreaming form with his body.

That's when she tickled him. "Gotcha!" she cried, as awake as could be.

"Faker," he said, grabbing her hands. "I should've known your sleeping was too convenient. You just wanted to tease."

Laughing, she stretched out from under him, tossing off her blanket at the same time she came to a stand. He sought the overhang behind the chair, motioning for her to come back.

"You're getting soaked!" he said.

"What's to hide from?"

Murphy didn't have an answer. But if he did, it'd be stuck in his throat.

Unlike her usual busy wardrobe, she was wearing a simple, white poet-type nightgown that came to midthigh. Along with her hair, it was already wet, clinging to her slim body as she leaned back her head to catch the rain in her mouth. He caught a peek of flesh through the thin material, glimpsed the dark pink of her nipples as they hardened.

"Come on, Kyle!" she said, laughing, gesturing to him. "It feels great!"

But he was nice and dry and, to be perfectly frank, admiring the performance too much to interrupt it by moving. He sat down and leaned back against the glass of the sliding door, arms on his knees. Lust thudded through him, like music through stereo speakers about to explode.

She seemed to recognize his appreciation, but all too soon her giddy look faded into something more serious. The kind of expression a woman got when she knew you were going to kiss her, when she knew a certain line had been crossed and she was inviting you to go a little farther.

That look almost tore Murphy into pieces, and he had to suck in a quick breath just to keep himself together.

"It's getting colder," he said over the spill of the rain. He got to his feet and held out his hand. "Let's get inside."

For a moment he thought she wasn't going to move at all. Thought that maybe he'd disappointed her by refusing to come out and play in the rain.

Kyle would've joined in the fun, dammit. Yet it was too late now to correct this slip-up. The split second when he should've joined her had passed.

He'd blown his chance to shake off his day at the law firm—which had been full of requests to "Do this research, Murphy," "I need this brief edited in two hours, Murphy." During a meeting he'd sat next to the man whose house he'd visited only last night. The man Murphy had convinced, during a water-cooler talk, that he'd been at the party but had to leave early. It'd been another small rush, Murphy thought. And right at this moment he'd just trashed his chance to experience one that would have been much more thrilling.

But the worst thing about it was her reaction. Even this little glimpse at his real personality—the boring guy with responsibilities to uphold—had brought a crashing halt to her good time.

So he overcame his wounded response and whole-heartedly became Kyle again, throwing himself back into the charade.

With pleasure.

He held out his hand to her one more time, losing himself in the aggressive grin he knew she wanted.

"Let me dry you off, Tam," he said, voice strangled.

Still, even as she came to him, her smile resurrecting itself in a saucy curve, his conscience—his Murphy side—remained.

And that conscience was telling "Kyle" to take it easy with this woman who'd started to get under his skin.

AFTER PROMISING TAM he'd be right back, Kyle had run downstairs, through the front door and outside. He'd gone to retrieve a bottle of wine, so Tam lingered in her bathroom in front of the mirror, where she was madly cleaning the counter of makeup and beauty aids that she'd left out.

Holding back a yawn—sleepiness *was* taking hold, but she wasn't about to give in to it—she fluffed up her hair, wishing it looked a lot less like a wet furball. And her nightie, which she just now realized was way skimpier than what she was usually comfortable wearing around other people, was saturated, but she refused to strip it off. *Yet.* It was for good reason: Kyle had said he was going to dry her, and she was definitely going to hold him to that.

As she busied herself getting towels for them, she could barely hold back her excitement. See, she thought, her faith in Kyle had paid off—it hadn't even taken a day for him to contact her again, even if it was after midnight. So what if it was—jeez, was it?—a booty call. She'd gotten him where she wanted him—with *her*. She was a winner as far as she was concerned.

Downstairs, the front door closed, charging her pulse into overdrive. She quickly took a hit of mouthwash, then hid the bottle back under the sink while he climbed the steps. Unable to stop herself, she yawned again, promising it would be the last time.

"I already got the wineglasses and opener and put them on my nightstand," she called as she heard him enter the room.

From the sound of it, he'd taken off his shoes, and she appreciated his courtesy. Actually, his thoughtfulness surprised her, because Kyle seemed like the type who would track mud into a house.

She heard him working the cork out of the bottle. "We'll let it breathe a little. You into wine?" he asked.

"I'd like to learn more about it. I've always meant to take a class or something." *Would you just get in here, Kyle?* she thought. *I'm wai-ting.*

As if summoned, he came, but only halfway. She caught his gaze in the mirror as he leaned against the door frame, all lean muscle and hardness under a T-shirt that'd suffered from only the slightest of rain. His eyes startled her with their vivid color—gray clouds against the night blue that waited outside her windows. He grinned, and warmth spread through her limbs like streaks of dawn flushing the sky.

"That was some rain dance of yours," he said, his faint lilt more obvious during this lazy moment.

"Nothing like it. I kind of feel—" she increased the wattage of her smile "—cleansed."

With sudden clarity, she realized how true that was. She felt new around Kyle. Reborn.

He still hadn't moved away from that door frame. Sheesh.

Tam took matters into her own hands and grabbed a thick towel, allowing it to unfurl as she turned to him. "But I'm not the only one who needs some drying."

"You first." He reached for the cloth.

"No, no. It's my turn to initiate some trouble." She crooked her finger at him. "Get over here."

His gaze enjoyed a leisurely trip over her body, taking in the fact that she wasn't wearing anything under her nightie.

Something seemed to flicker in his eyes, as if a fuse had blown. Grin widening, he straightened away from the door frame, grabbed the bottom of his shirt with his arms crossed and peeled it off.

She caught a glimpse of the thin, dark trail of hair that disappeared into his jeans; the honed abs that would provide a bumpy ride when she skimmed her fingers over them; the wide chest sprinkled with hair; the arms bunched with streamlined muscles.

Tam clutched that towel, her knees liquefying. Yow. She swallowed, then managed a sentence. "Just toss your shirt anywhere."

He did, mouth tilted as he kept measuring her reaction. Jerk. He knew she was buzzing for him.

In feisty response to his arrogance, she casually

stood on tiptoe and began drying his hair with rough strokes. Laughing softly, he accommodated her by bending. As she came to his neck, she forgot herself, slowed down, exploring him.

She could practically feel the warmth emanating from his skin. More than anything, she wanted it against hers.

"Your house," he said, breaking the sudden tension. "It's great. You're decorating the interior yourself?"

She blushed at the mention of the half-finished rooms that didn't coalesce into any certain theme. It had the effect of an experimental canvas that wasn't painted with any thought as to the overall picture. Sometimes she wondered if this said too much about her: indecisiveness about what she was, a major fear of settling on a definitive identity.

"I'm working with different styles," she said, settling on the safe answer. "A little bit of this, a little bit of that."

"You're very creative. Your clothes, your designing…"

With even more deliberation, she began drying his arms, lingering over the smooth beauty of them, wanting to feel them enclosing her. "It started when I was a kid. I used to make these shoebox dioramas—bedrooms, living rooms, parlors. My dad would always trip over them because I left so many on the floors."

"Do you design for your job now?"

She eased his arm up, slipping the towel over his chest and thrilling at how his nipples went hard. These past nights, he'd done the same thing to her with merely a passing touch or even a seductive sentence. Returning the favor was just as enticing.

"I work in a cubicle at Dillard Marketing downtown. You probably don't remember my saying that during our first phone call because it's so inconsequential. Basically, I punch numbers into a computer all day. I'm a temp so…" So what? Did she know where it went from there? "Well, that's not where I'm going to be by next summer, that's for sure."

"Then you're going to go into designing."

He'd framed it as a statement. Jeez, he actually sounded confident that this would be an easy transition for her. It almost made her believe in the same dream.

Tam didn't say anything for a minute, instead concentrating on his stomach. His muscles flinched with each circle of the towel. Every movement made her more and more aware of him—the acceleration of his breathing, the way he grabbed on to the wall rack for support.

She walked around to his rear, dabbed the cotton up his back. Her movements weren't so much sexual as…intimate. As if they were used to standing in a bathroom while chatting with each other and touching like this.

Intimacy. Not in the plan, Tam.

"So you're going to quit by summer?" he continued. "You must have a better job lined up."

She wished. "I'm not really sure what I'm going to do. All I know is that I made a deal with myself to get it together before then. You know, start my real life and all that. I had this notion that I could find *the* perfect career, something that would make me happy and would put my interests to use. I don't know…a job that wasn't 'a job.' Something that would make me wake up in the morning with a smile on my face because I'd be doing something fulfilling, something that'd preserve my individuality and idealism, I suppose."

"Wouldn't that be great?"

Longing weighed down his voice, but when he suddenly shot her a grin, she didn't take his tone seriously.

"My plan also includes moving out of this house," she added.

"Why the hell would you want to do that?"

"For starters, I told my dad I would."

"He's coming back?"

"I don't know. It's just that I'm determined to move to my own place because I can't leech off him forever."

Why were they talking about all this? She was surprised he even cared. After all, this was supposed to be just a fling.

"Boy, aren't you just full of the questions tonight," she said, just to ease them back to where they should be: in bed, with a minimum of revelations or deep conversation.

He paused at that, then laughed with a hint of something that threw her off balance: shyness. A twist in the Kyle she thought she'd sort-of known.

Determined to get back to familiar ground, she reached around his waist to undo his jeans. They weren't that wet, but ask her if she cared.

"Wait," Kyle said, holding her hands in his and guiding her to the front of him. "How old are you again?"

They'd exchanged ages during that first call—Kyle was twenty-seven; she was two years younger. Obviously he didn't have a wonderful talent for remembering details; she could imagine him joining the ranks of anniversary-forgetting men who slept in the doghouse. Typical guy.

"I'm twenty-five," she said.

"Still a pup." He glanced down at her with a mix of fondness and amusement. But the concoction disappeared quickly. "You've got a lot of time before you need to settle down, Tam. Is your dad kicking you out?"

"No, no, no. He's perfectly content to work like a maniac and travel all over the U.S. collecting houses like this one. He has three, but he lives in the New York place since that's where he's consulting now. In fact, I think he's glad this one's getting some use. But…" How could she explain that the walls closed in on her whenever she realized that this wasn't her own home, that her dad could come back at any time and justifiably tell her to paint the house back to the colors he liked? "Well, I'm the one who's forcing the move. I just feel it's time to get on with my own thing, that's all."

She didn't want to add that the thought of depending on someone else had come to stifle her, especially over the past few months of travel and reflection; after all, she'd come to the philosophical conclusion that you should count on *yourself* and no one else to survive. Her mom, who never called, who rarely even sent birthday cards, was living proof that other people were unreliable and fickle. Being on her own during the backpacking trip had taught her that she could, indeed, live on her own. And the Europe excursion—which her dad had funded as last year's Christmas gift—had changed her life in other ways, too. Her friends had never allowed her to forget who'd paid her way, and after one joke too many about her "leeching," she'd come to the San Fran home determined to change that.

She just needed to save enough money to be able to do it, was all. Her very *own* money.

She must've been wearing some kind of sorry expression, because Kyle was looking at her with unnerving sympathy. Maybe he wasn't skillful at retaining details, but he could read between her lines with a keen perceptiveness she hadn't before given him credit for.

For a second he seemed confused about something, agitated. But then he brushed past her, securing the other towel. With movements that felt more comforting than seductive, he removed the nightie from her body, keeping his eyes averted for some reason.

The tone of their interaction seemed to grow quieter, into something that reintroduced that intimacy she'd been trying to avoid. As he tossed away the nightie, the rustle of the material echoed throughout the small, silent room. She just stood there, naked as the day in front of him.

Slowly she met his gaze, expecting to find undiluted lust in his eyes now. Expecting that her bared body would shake him up and bring back the man who was supposed to be as empty and tasty as junk food for her system.

But something puzzling remained in his eyes. Something that scared her because he seemed removed or concerned or…she wasn't sure what.

He began drying her hair, soothing her with the low, sexy voice that had decorated her fantasies for the past few nights. "Sounds like you're putting a lot of pressure on yourself, Tam."

She nodded, closing her eyes, feeling drugged as his towel-covered hands massaged the rain from her hair.

"I know someone like that, too," he said, his voice distant. "A cousin."

He dabbed at her face, as if he were drying the

remnants of a bad dream away. Then he smoothed the cloth over her ears, her neck, her arms, more caring than she'd ever have guessed he could be. Discreetly, she yawned again, swaying under the motion of his hands.

Why wasn't he attacking her right now? He was barely even *looking*.

"He works probably as hard as your dad does," Kyle continued. "Never takes much of a break because his parents expect the world from him. Actually, he's made a career out of pleasing everyone. I…kind of pity him."

Tam opened her eyes, finding a faraway look in his gaze. When he saw that she'd noticed, he put on a grin. His sudden jauntiness clashed with the moment.

And when he saw that she wasn't buying it, the grin disappeared. He avoided her glance, concentrating instead on gliding the towel downward. Crouching, he rubbed her legs, pausing. Then, with sudden stilted efficiency, he moved up, between her thighs. As a pierce of desire dug into her, Tam planted her hands on his shoulders, tilting back her head.

"Kyle…"

He stopped. Stood. Tossed the towel away and grabbed a dry one to wrap around her body.

"How about we get to that wine?" he asked, already on his way out the door.

Wha…how…?

Why had he come here if it wasn't for some sex?

Then she remembered the masquerade, the slow games they'd played with each other to draw out the sensations.

That's obviously the way he liked it, and that's the way it would be for tonight, too, huh?

All right. But not for long, she hoped.

She wandered out to her half-finished, baroque bedroom, with its gauze-draped bed and gilded-mirror essence. Very *Scarlet Pimpernel,* if she said so herself. And the shirtless man standing near her mattress was just as confusing as the deceptive hero of the novel she'd read in literature class years ago.

While pouring the wine, Kyle grinned at her again. Now the gesture didn't seem as forced, thank goodness. They could do with some of the old playfulness.

"Your tastes run to the effusive," he said.

"Wow, a waiter who uses the word *effusive.* Do you read the dictionary at night?"

He laughed and barely avoided spilling the beverage. With a touché nod, he gave her the glass. She crawled onto the bed with it, facing him while reclining against the massive pillows in a none-too-subtle hint.

"I…had a hell of an English teacher in high school." He took a considering sip of the wine, made a face that said it passed muster, then wandered over to the fireplace. When he saw it was electric, he fired it up and held his hands out to the flames.

She left him to conduct his tease, sipping her vino and feeling the dance of the fire's heat over her skin. That, along with the rubdown and the late hour, encouraged the return of the yawns. But she was going to stay up for this, you betcha.

Yup, anytime now, Kyle…

"Second Bay-Area Tradition," he said, referring to the house's style. He sounded a mile away, wrapped in fog. "You and your dad have good taste."

"Mmm-hmm." With fingers anchored on the stem, she balanced the wineglass on her chest; she'd almost drained it, anyway.

"These older houses are really well built…."

This wasn't seduction talk. But Tam wasn't minding so much. She liked hearing his voice fill the room. It made the space so much less lonely, less in need of color and frills.

Soon—she didn't know how much later—she felt the glass being taken from her, felt the mattress dip with his weight, felt her flesh warm with the proximity of his.

She cuddled into him, breathing in the clean lime of his soap and skin. Her mouth settled against his chest, and she slipped her leg between the both of his. As if reading her wishes, he wrapped an arm around her, his muscles firm and perfectly fitted to her curves.

Before Tam drifted off, she thought she heard him say something about staying just a little bit longer until he really, *really* had to leave.

But it sounded like the sort of lie she'd tell herself, too, so she let it float off into the ether of her sleep.

8

Murphy woke up with his arms empty the next morning and, for a scattered second, he wasn't sure where he was or what he was doing there.

But then everything came crashing back to him when Tam bustled into the room.

Through the sheers that hung from her bed, he could see she was running around like a dervish, dressed in a tamer-than-usual version of her quirky wardrobe: a turquoise, form-fitting skirt and shirt with American Indian flair. But she was moving so quickly he never caught the details.

"Oh, good, you're awake," she said, fixing an earring as she disappeared into the bathroom. Once inside, her voice was muffled. "You can eat what's in the fridge. And my front door locks by itself. I can't believe I forgot to set my alarm!"

Shit.

Sitting bolt upright, he scanned the room for a clock and found a gilded one on the fireplace mantel. 9:04.

"Late," he muttered, tossing off the covers he'd somehow crawled under last night. He caught a whiff of Tam's scent and was struck with heated dizziness. But he fought it—he had to if he wanted to get to the firm before the day was wasted.

Dammit, Murphy had never been late a day in his life, and he cursed himself for being so careless. Yet, oddly, getting back home or setting an alarm clock hadn't been a priority when he'd fallen asleep with Tam cuddled against him last night.

Hey. Cuddled?

With a whoosh of remembrance, he realized that nothing had even happened between them. Nada. Zip. Not even when Tam had been standing in front of him without a stitch of clothing on.

The image filtered into him, brushing away everything else but the sight of her flushed skin; breasts that were the perfect size for his palms; a slim waist; a patch of sable that had made his mouth water.

For a guy who'd come over for a sexual fix, he'd sure blown it. He'd driven here as Kyle but had ended up as Murphy. Yeah, sure, he'd been as tempted as hell to continue where they'd left off at the masquerade, but then Tam had started talking about personal things like ambitions. There'd been real anguish in her expression, and no matter how much Murphy wanted her, his conscience wouldn't allow him to take advantage of that.

So he'd argued with his insistent lust by telling himself that they had all night, that he didn't need to initiate anything while she was looking so vulnerable. And he had kept repeating it, over and over, until the wine and the late hour had gotten to Tam and to him, too.

Right now his inner Kyle was kicking him. *Nice timing,* it said. *You give all of us guys in the dog pound a bad name with your damned consideration, Murph.*

Male pride gnawed at Murphy. Oh, yeah? Well, this wasn't over yet. Don't count him out.

That daredevil thrill glowed in his chest, expanding and taking over again. She wasn't all soft and seemingly in need of protection now.

He found himself relaxing, resting his arms on his knees. "Don't go to work," he said loudly enough for her to hear him in the bathroom. As the idea of playing hooky set in, he allowed Kyle's grin to spread over his mouth.

A beat passed. Then Tam poked her head out. He could see her hair was wet from a shower, wound into a mound of drying curls and turquoise clips. The color matched her wide eyes.

"I've got a report due today," she said hesitantly, even though it looked as if she thought it was a fine idea. "I can't—"

"I'll make you breakfast." He glanced at the clock, shrugged. "Make that brunch, by the time it's done. There're some recipes I learned from the New Orleans side of the family." No lie there. While getting schooled at Tulane, he'd picked up some mean cooking tricks from his great-aunt and, back home, had taught them to the real Kyle, the fool who thought they both could open their own restaurant one day.

He felt comfortable telling her the part about the cooking and Gulf side of the family. It was a personal nugget of information, but a safe one.

"How Renaissance of you," Tam said, coming all the way out of the bathroom. She was holding a brush that he thought might be for blush, not that she really needed it. "I'll bet you're more of a cook than my own macaroni-and-cheese-makin' self. No wonder you talk about opening your own place."

"My cousin and I kid each other about it, but he

doesn't think I can commit to something like owning a business, and besides…" Murphy battled a frown, getting some perspective from Kyle's point of view. "He'd never take a chance like that."

"This is the cousin you talked about before? The one who makes 'a career out of pleasing everyone'?"

Murphy swallowed, forcing himself to go on. "That's the one. If he deviated from what our family expects of him…well, that wouldn't go over too well with anyone."

Especially the real Murphy.

Tam held the brush away from her face, taking in the information. Then she shrugged. "I'm sure he's a big boy. If he wanted to change his life, he would."

God, she made it sound easy. But she hadn't factored in the crushed disappointment his parents would suffer or the pressure he was under to pay them back for all the opportunities they'd given him. Family was one of the most important things in the world, and letting them down was as appealing as cutting off his own nose. And as unthinkable.

Tam laughed. "Funny, but… I think I know more about this cousin of yours than you."

Whoa! Before Murphy reacted, he caught himself, recovering just in time.

"Not that it's a bad thing," Tam added, holding up her hands, probably thinking she'd gone too far outside their penciled boundaries. "I mean, that's not what we're about."

What exactly *are* we about? he wanted to ask, but the question was directed more at himself, so it was useless to utter it aloud.

Tam brushed at a cheekbone, the gesture somehow coming off as stiff. "Talking just complicates what we agreed on. Don't you think?"

Was she testing him? Wanting him to commit to something? Or was she regretting how much she'd revealed last night and letting him know it?

He affably spread out his hands. No harm, no foul. "Maybe we'd do best to express ourselves in other ways from now on?" he asked, summoning Kyle's charm.

She gave a pert nod, and Murphy translated that as relief that he'd gone along with it. A pinch of something that he couldn't identify nagged at him.

"Then we're on the same page," he added.

Tam tossed her brush at the bathroom. Murphy wasn't sure where it landed, but the resulting clatter told him it couldn't be where it belonged.

She didn't seem to mind as she sidled closer to him.

Morning breath, Murphy thought. What was Kyle's policy on that? Ignore it for a good-morning-sunshine kiss?

In response to the way he automatically shifted away from her, Tam halted, putting her hands on her hips. "All right. I'm just going to come out with it. What's the deal, Kyle?"

He tried to look innocent. Deal? Who? Him? What?

"First," she pointed to the bathroom, "I stand in front of you last night as naked as a jaybird and you put a towel around me. Then," she pointed to the bed, "I wait for you to jump on me and you stand by the fire like *it's* all you came here for. And can I mention what happened after the masquerade when you wanted to go home instead of staying with me? I'm confused. You call me again and come over to my house, but when you get here, you barely even touch me. You're hot and cold. And I'm talking pretty, pretty, pretty hot, too.....

He thought some toothpaste could solve this momentary hesitation-to-kiss-her debacle, but how could he explain the rest of it? Especially since he didn't understand what was happening himself.

"Do you have a girlfriend or something?" she asked. "I know guys like that, and they do everything but actually have intercourse with another woman, and that way they can tell their significant others that they were faithful in some warped technical way. Somehow, the oh-I-didn't-actually-screw-her story makes sense to them. Are you one of those, Kyle?"

From her expression, he wondered if she'd encountered one or two of these creeps.

"No," he said, scooting away from her a bit more. "I don't have a girlfriend."

"Then…" She shook her head, searching for another explanation for how he could come off as so randy but be so damned slow about it. It only took seconds for her mouth to shape into an *O*.

He rolled his eyes. "No, I'm not gay, either." Good God.

"It's cool. I thought maybe you might be experimenting…?"

"*No.*"

"Then what's the problem?"

She had this look on her face, as if she'd run out of excuses for him and was turning inward for an explanation.

"Tam." Murphy started to inch toward her, then remembered the curse of morning breath. That's when he spotted his untouched glass of wine.

So he held up a finger and quaffed some of it, swishing it around in his mouth and swallowing.

There.

He got up from the bed and, as he came toward her, she flicked a relieved glance to the glass, probably knowing what he'd been doing with it. Maybe even understanding why he hadn't pulled her to the bed and begun undressing her at first sight.

Taking her face in his hands, Murphy shook his head. "I want you so bad it's driving me into the ground." He felt himself floating into Kyle territory again, pulled into the quickened heartbeat of the moment. He had something to prove after backing off last night. "The towel drying was just foreplay that we were too tired to complete."

Her gaze had gone fuzzy, and that revved him to a higher level of need—one he hadn't allowed himself to access since the other night.

For better or worse, he welcomed it back.

"You sure like to stretch things out and make me wait." She reached out to press her hand against his stomach.

His cock rammed awake. "Why don't you stay home from work and we'll take care of that?"

The instant she closed her eyes and leaned back her head, he knew he'd lost her.

"The team I support is putting together a big presentation that's due tomorrow."

What'd happened to the free spirit he thought she was? "There's no orgasm in 'team,' you know."

"They're giving the presentation *tomorrow,* Kyle."

"Hey—" he ran his thumb over her mouth, her lower lip "—I thought there was no future in this job for you."

Against his stomach, she bunched her hand. He thought he had her again, and his body tightened, expectant and jubilant.

But then he caught her running a gaze over the walls: the intricate borders near the ceiling, the work she'd probably spent hours on. He remembered that this wasn't her own house.

What she'd told him last night returned full force: *I just feel it's time to move on with my own thing.*

Maybe she had to make sacrifices to remain that free spirit.

"There's no future at Dillard," she said softly, backing away from him, "but there's a paycheck."

She didn't have to say the rest. One more day of pay would get her that much closer to her goal of getting her life together by next summer. He didn't know why that was so important, but it obviously trumped him.

And why shouldn't it?

"This doesn't mean I don't want your home cookin' though," she said, already backing toward the door as if she didn't trust herself to stop moving away from him.

Should he promise her another night? This couldn't continue…or could it?

Hell, would it be that big a deal to stretch this out for another twenty-four hours? And based on her recognition of this no-strings-attached fling, she wasn't expecting anything more than to get laid and to move on when it got old.

Why couldn't he do that, too? She was inviting him in, for God's sake.

Adrenaline took him over…the heady craving, the need.

Before he could revert to logic, he answered.

"How about nine o'clock?" he asked. "I'm off work tonight, but I've got something I can't get out of until then."

"Nine o'clock." She grabbed on to the doorjamb, as if it was a rail that was keeping her from being sucked back to him.

Maybe it was his imagination, but he thought that her cheeks had become more pink. That her eyes had glimmered just a little more *effusively*.

Yet…nah. Sex buddies didn't get emotionally invested.

As if proving him right, she blew him a light kiss, then left.

But after he heard the front door close, Murphy was on the phone to the firm, calling in sick for the very first time in his life, even if he didn't have to play hooky for Tam anymore.

He was taking just one step farther away from the man he was expected to be.

And it felt good.

"YOUR JAMBALAYA SUCKS," Kyle said to Murphy as they commandeered the kitchen of Bridget Sullivan.

Lost in thoughts of what later tonight would bring, Murphy barely heard Kyle. He was sautéing the onions, celery, green pepper and garlic that were required for one of his favorite dishes, focusing on how this was literally a rehearsal for the food he'd be cooking Tam.

If not for family responsibilities, he'd be at her place by now, burying himself in her. Every tick of the clock over the stove emphasized that.

But he'd promised his mom dinner tonight because she'd guilted him into it. She was still on her kick about him and Kyle not talking enough.

Kyle was in charge of the gumbo and fried okra, whipping up the roux at the stove while commenting on every move Murphy made while he took care of the jambalaya and bread pudding. Par for the course. In the kitchen, as with many other things, they were always pacing each other.

When Murphy didn't respond to Kyle's prodding, his cousin tried another tack, just to get Murphy's goat. "I hear you didn't show up for work today. And, in other related news, hell froze over."

Behind them, his mom's voice rang out like a gong. "Kyle Sullivan, you wash your mouth out. There'll be no mention of that sort of inferno in my home."

Murphy didn't have to turn around to see that his mom would be hiding a smile as she darted out of the room with her hands full of dishes. She was whippet thin, with rosy cheeks, black hair streaked with gray and eyes that matched the blue of the most beautiful silks she worked with in the tailor shop his parents had owned for twenty years.

Murphy just shook his head, eager to get back into his thoughts and fantasies of Tam.

"No problem, I can win her over again." Kyle kept stirring, as was required for the roux. "Anyway, aren't you going to answer me? Why'd you stay home today? I thought it'd take Armageddon for that to happen."

"Food poisoning, I think." The lie slipped easily from his tongue. It was becoming simple.

It was almost horrifying.

Almost.

"Man, you've been eating your own food. Didn't I say your cooking sucked?" Kyle pointed to Murphy's concoction. "Proof is right there."

Hot kisses, soft skin, sweet moans and sighs... Murphy was too far gone inside his head to engage Kyle.

It didn't take long for his cousin to back off and stop yapping. And soon, as they put the finishing touches on their dishes—having weaved around each other with ease because they'd cooked together often enough—Murphy actually came out of his sexual fog long enough to notice Kyle's frown.

What was it with him? Was he pissed at Murphy for ignoring him?

Everyone settled in at the table. Unlike Sunday brunch, when all of the family got together, including Kyle's three sisters and their families, it was just the four of them: Mom, Dad and the boys.

Ah, yes, Mom the Peacemaker, he thought, casting a glance at her as they finished saying grace. She was trying hard to smooth the recent friction between him and Kyle. With her almost preternatural senses, she'd somehow ascertained that her charges had found themselves in a bigger conflict than ever before.

"Pass the jambalaya," Dad bellowed from the head of the table. Like his wife, he was in good shape. They were California seniors, filling their weekends and days off with church work and hikes in Golden Gate Park.

Grudgingly, Kyle passed Murphy's dish to the uncle who'd raised him.

"Ian tells me you were off sick today," Murphy's mom said.

Kyle heaped spoonfuls of gumbo into a bowl, as if setting an example he hoped everyone would follow. "Food poisoning."

"Food poisoning?" Mom held a hand to her chest.

"From last night. I was just getting over it. I'm fine now." Murphy took some jambalaya and dug in, focusing on his meal so he wouldn't have to talk.

"What did you eat?"

Murphy swallowed his mouthful, smiled at his mom. "Don't worry."

"Fast food," muttered his dad. "That stuff'll kill you."

The older man sniffed at Kyle's gumbo. Across the table, Murphy clearly saw his cousin sit up in his chair.

Then, when Dad took some, Kyle grinned.

"A shame," Mom said. "You were the only employee never to have used a sick day, Murphy."

And he'd been the only kid in school who'd never needed her to write absence notes.

Still, it sounded like her pride in him had taken a hit, and Murphy flinched at the thought of that.

"It's one day, Bridget," his dad said. "Murphy's not the type to go beyond that."

"But, Gerald—"

"It won't happen again." His dad saluted him with his spoon. "Not with our Murphy, because one day he's going to make partner in a firm even more prestigious than Ian's, and he knows how important it is to keep himself healthy and on top of his game."

Like mist, Murphy's future formed into a vision before his eyes. The life of a drone, up at dawn and into the office until night, was well set in motion.

An automaton, he thought. The last kind of guy a fun lover like Tam Clarkson would go for.

"I'm in line for a raise," Kyle said.

Stirring his gumbo, Murphy glanced up at his cousin. Was he trying to save Murphy from this grilling?

"That's good," his dad said, gaze still on Murphy. "Real good, Kyle. Say, Murph, you get your results for the bar yet?"

His parents liked to check every day, and Murphy always said the same thing. "Still waiting. And I will be for about another month."

Across the table, Kyle stirred his gumbo, silent.

Maybe he hadn't been trying to run interference for Murphy at all. It was no secret that Kyle had grown up idolizing his older cousin, and maybe the comment about his raise had just been a way for him to remind his parental figures that he was succeeding, too. Sure, he'd never be a lawyer, but a guy needed validation every once in a while.

Murphy jerked his chin at him. "Are they giving you the private dining room?"

A small smile lit over Kyle's mouth. "Next week."

"Nice."

Kyle looked up, and Murphy saw the gratitude in his expression. He also saw that Kyle realized he wasn't even near being entirely excused from what he'd done to Tam. Nope, *that* still remained between them like an elephant that was squatting on the table.

Little did Kyle know, though, that Murphy couldn't

drop the Tam episode because it reminded him too much of what a hypocrite *he* was.

"Hopefully," his mom said, interrupting the silence, "we'll get good news on the bar this time."

"Eh, Murph?" his dad added.

He merely nodded, knowing how concerned they'd been when he'd initially failed it. It put a bad taste in his mouth, and it wasn't from the food.

All his self-doubt had settled in the back of his throat—the mortification of not living up to his potential, the suspicion that maybe, just maybe, he'd not done his best on the exam for a reason that was too disturbing to acknowledge.

He'd *wanted* to pass the bar, for God's sake. Stupid to even think he'd sabotaged himself, given himself a good reason not to pursue a career that was sucking the life out of him.

"He'll pass, Uncle Gerald, don't sweat it," Kyle said, almost causing Murphy to fall out of his chair.

He didn't even meet Murphy's stunned look as he launched into a topic clearly designed to distract his dad: the 49ers and their chances for the Superbowl. Meanwhile, Murphy's parents did what they did for every Murphy-and-Kyle-cooked dinner: closed their eyes in appreciation.

Murphy didn't have to be told: it was damned good.

Still, he forgot all about the satisfaction of making an exceptional meal.

Had Kyle actually been defending Murphy or was football talk his method of getting Dad's and Mom's attention off the family overachiever?

Whatever it was, Murphy was thankful.

And, as his cousin talked and talked in his animated style, Murphy took notes.

Thinking what he'd give to be Kyle again.

And to get back over to Tam's just as soon as possible.

9

IT HAD TRIED TAM to her limits to wait until nine o'clock for dinner. She was an early-bird kind of girl when it came to eating. Late meals weren't good for her diet and wreaked havoc on her sleep.

But Kyle's meal had been worth the wait. Seriously. Interrupted sleeping habits or not, his cooking was divine.

Right now they were lounging in the living room, finishing up his version of bread pudding—it was laced with amaretto and was giving Tam fits of joy.

Not much money had been needed to decorate the room in French country style: white paint that had been artistically tampered with to seem cracked; heavy, thick wood around the square windows; lanterns lighting the area in dim romanticism; wooden bowls, some filled with fruit and some with herbs.

As Tam lay back on a pile of large pillows that were encased in peasant-patterned materials, she watched Kyle going through her CD collection beside the hutch that hid the stereo. He looked hot, dressed in jeans and a dark-blue T, looking fresh and clean.

She, herself, had taken a bath earlier, after getting off the phone with one of her college buddies. Her skin was scented and glowing in readiness for whatever arose tonight.

No secret as to what she was hoping *that* would be.

"That was…jeez, incredible." She rubbed a palm over her stomach. Waves of contentment forced a small sound of pleasure from her, even if she was still starving in a much different way. "You know, if you did open your own restaurant, there'd be a line around the corner."

"This is nothing. You should taste the food in New Orleans."

"Someday." Her hand sketched a little lower, from her stomach to her lower belly. As she watched him, she increased the pressure of her touch. Blood rushed between her legs. "It's too bad I didn't make it there before the hurricanes did."

He paused, pensive. "If any town can come back from trouble, it's that place. Believe me. It'll be back to normal in no time." He seemed to snap out of it, shooting her his patented charm-laden grin. "You're sure the traveler, huh?"

It seemed to cost him a second while he took in her position: sprawled over the pillows, one hand tucked beneath her head, the other moving over her belly.

For a moment he didn't move. He merely white-knuckled the CD case he was holding, the dark center of his eyes consuming the blue of his irises.

Teasing him, she slipped farther down her big pillow, causing her oversize beige shirt to tighten over her breasts. Oddly enough, the wardrobe choice wasn't flashy, and she was surprised to realize that she felt comfortable enough around Kyle not to need all the bells and whistles she used around others.

Tonight she'd chosen not to wear a bra, so the friction stimulated her nipples. She knew he would be able to see the nubby outlines of them through the material. The sinuous feel of cotton over her sensitized tips made her shift restlessly, her long shimmery skirt riding up her knees ever so slightly.

Boldly, she guided her hand between her legs, then moaned.

That did it. He tossed away the CD case, ambled over to her, arms curved out at his sides, chest rising and falling with labored breaths.

Lust churned deep inside her while she tugged up her dress to her thighs and smoothed her hands up and down them.

It was going to happen—a replay of the masquerade.

As "The Humming Chorus" from *Madame Butterfly* quietly sang through the speakers, Kyle hovered above her. He was barefoot, comfortable in her house, and the realization unsettled Tam even while it turned her on.

Lying alongside her, he placed a hand over one of hers. She led him below her skirt, then turned on her side to face him, arm under her head again to cushion it.

As he stroked her, she opened up for him, biting her lower lip. They listened to the flutes, violins and human voices winding together in graceful staccato and tragic counterpoint.

"You ever seen this?" she asked softly. *"Madame Butterfly?"*

Kyle pressed his thumb against her center, and she let out a low sound of satisfaction.

"Do I come off like an opera kind of guy?"

Slowly she coasted a gaze down his body, back up again. When she reached his face, his eyes were shining with amusement.

"You know," she said, "one second I think I know you, the next I'm believing you're a different breed altogether."

He glanced away. "That's what makes people interesting. Unexpected sides, secrets you find out about them bit by bit."

He wouldn't be around long enough for bit by bit. Dammit.

Frustrated, she slowly sat up, her motion removing his hand from between her legs. Without comment, she reached for a glass of wine she'd set on an end table—a red Bordeaux. As a waiter, Kyle would know enough to appreciate the vintage. She assumed he worked in a high-end restaurant.

Kyle took hold of her skirt and pulled at it. "Hey."

"Hey, what?" Reverting to everything-is-all-right girl, Tam gestured flippantly to him with the glass. The red juices seesawed with the motion. Then she drank again, just to keep herself from getting all needy on him.

She hated putting on an act. But her actions were established by a pattern of abandonment, and she didn't know what else to do.

In spite of the rejection she'd been through—or maybe because of it—all she wanted was to feel someone holding her and appreciating her, even if it was just for a short time.

Tam corrected herself. *Especially* if it was for a short time. Relationships weren't a priority at this point, but the facsimile of one would sure be nice. And a fling guaranteed a neat, clean ending where no one would actually do any rejecting.

At least, that was the idea.

His gaze was steady, almost as if he was trying to look past her surface and into her most closely guarded thoughts. She flinched, the first one to look away this time. In the background, an aria played.

"I know what you need," he said, rolling up to a stand in one easy move. "Wait here."

He left the room for the dining area. He knew what she needed? Sure. If he did, he'd get back here right now.

When he reentered the room with a plastic tarp, which she'd been using to catch the paint from a mural on the dining room wall, her heart flickered, hope rekindling.

She couldn't resist him; what had made her think it would be possible?

He grinned at her, spreading the plastic over the floor. Then he jerked his chin at the wine she was holding, and her blood began to roar to the center of her body because she thought she knew what he had in mind.

"Your skirt," Kyle said. "Take it off."

On a note of disbelief, she laughed.

Still, she couldn't deny him this game, so she pushed her skirt down her legs, kicking out of it.

Immediately, his body went taut, his gaze burning from her face downward. He looked as if he was primed to explode.

Jarred into motion, he shucked off his T-shirt. In the lantern light, amber slashes of flame coated the smoothness of his chest, the sleek muscles.

Oh, now, this was something that could make her forget their tenuous situation.

He went over to his glass of wine and took a casual sip.

Brutal heat consumed her. What would be next, and could she stand to wait for it?

With a low laugh, he resumed undressing with arrogant deliberation, unbuttoning his fly and taking off his jeans.

Her pulse skittered as he slid the denim down, revealing just how excited he was getting. At the sight of his rising erection, she let out a breath she hadn't even known she'd been holding. Yearning twisted between her thighs.

After nudging his jeans to the side, he went to pick up the wine bottle from the end table. "Come here."

She did, taking her time, meeting him at the center of the tarp. All her midnight fantasies sharpened into pinpricks over her flesh. She wanted to taste him, feel him against her lips, just as he'd felt her the other night.

"Kyle," she said, so into the game that she wanted to take over, "it's my turn now."

He smiled indulgently at the hunger in her tone. He looked as if he didn't want to give up control.

Determined, she moved nearer to him, oxygen thin in her lungs, mind reeling. Embers seemed to flit over her skin, reminding her that she shouldn't allow Kyle to get too far *under* it, even if she'd never felt this free and comfortable with a man before.

Carefully, she took the bottle from him and trickled a little wine over his chest. He hitched in a breath and gritted his jaw.

"My turn," she repeated. "I want this."

She bent, licked the liquid from the center of his ribs upward, tasting deep fruits, cedar—and skin.

When he clutched her shoulders, she knew he'd do this for her—allow her to be her own woman, let her prove to herself that she was as desirable as he made her think she might be.

After setting down the bottle, Tam took his glass, dipped her fingers into it, then lifted them to his mouth. She rubbed wine onto his lips, until he latched on, sucking at her fingers. Stabbed by longing, she started to push in and out, simulating what she wanted him to do to her later.

He groaned, laving her fingers with his tongue, his eyes closing.

She couldn't just stand there watching—not with fire rushing through her, gathering and pooling into needling sensation, engorging her into readiness.

Unable to stand it, she went to him, slipped her tongue into his mouth while removing her fingers. He kept up his own easy rhythm, and they devoured each other, a slow feasting.

He was hard against her belly, his penis digging into her flesh as the remaining wine from his chest dampened and stuck to her shirt.

But now it was her turn to make him wait.

With slick care, she disengaged her mouth from his. Her lips were wet with saliva and berries. His eyes were almost black with the intensity of his pupils.

She took her glass and poured the rest of the wine over one of his shoulders, his back, his chest. By the time she got to his other shoulder, there were only drips of red left. Negligently she bent down and rolled the glass to the far reaches of the tarp.

On her way back up, she dragged her hands up his wine-streaked calves, thighs. She hushed a breath over his penis, careful not to give him the satisfaction of her lips on it yet. Then she continued, caressing his hips, belly, ribs, nipples. He was sticky wet, and saliva gathered in her mouth at the thought of what she was about to do.

"Close your eyes," she said in his ear.

Under her fingertips, he shuddered. But he did what she asked.

She stepped away, wanting to drive him to his limits, just as he'd done to her.

But she was too eager to play out the game, and moments later, she quietly crept nearer. Against a soft overture from the stereo, wine dripped to the tarp.

Tap, tap, tap…

She used her tongue on his heel, pressing her mouth into a kiss. Kyle's leg jerked at the contact.

Laying her cheek against him, rubbing against leg hair and wined flesh, she asked, "Where's the next one going to be?"

"Damned if I know."

He sounded choked, and a rip of satisfaction tore at her.

Pulse pounding in her ears, she rose, held her breath, sneaking to her next target, the tarp bunching beneath her bare feet.

As she kissed his neck, he bucked. She smiled, drank the wine from him until that area of flesh was clean of it. Cherries, blackberries, the tannic hint of earthiness and spice.

"Next?" she whispered in his ear.

"Tam—"

"Shh." The ends of his hair wisped between her lips, tickling her. Need curdled in her belly, tightening.

She paused, listening to the tap of wine on tarp, the unevenness of his breathing, the beat of her body. Then, in a sneak attack, she lifted his arm and licked up the side of him until she got to his ribs. There, too, she drank off him, savoring his nipple, his collarbone, his neck.

When he tried to draw her against him, she stepped back, beyond control but grasping for it, anyway.

"Close your eyes again, Kyle."

"You're going to fry my brain."

By now, his erection was straining, bobbing away from his body. She was ready, also—was she ever—but she hadn't finished yet.

"I'm still thirsty," she said, bending to pick up the bottle. She took a long swallow, coating her dry mouth and throat.

He muttered something under his breath, yet he closed his eyes as commanded. Contentment hit her like an electric surge.

With cruel slowness, she poured more wine over his back, drinking it as it flowed. It splashed over her face, her shirt. Giddy, she saved the rest of it and ran her mouth down his spine, his butt. She nipped at him, right where the curve of his cheek met his leg, running her tongue in the crease there to sip up every last drop.

She continued with the rest of his body—except for one important part.

By the time she got to it, he was almost vibrating.

The wine was warm, she knew—as warm as her mouth would be.

She spilled the rest of the liquid over his penis, and he reached out to steady himself, gripping her shoulders. At that, she dropped the emptied bottle.

Without a word, she positioned herself in front of him, taking him into her mouth and imbibing the sweetness from the stem of his erection. Utterly liberated, she circled the tip of him, swirled down and sucked back up.

He gave a tight groan and held her head, encouraging her, letting her do whatever she wanted.

She moved to his balls, where wine dripped. Gently, she traced them until he groaned in anguish.

"Get over here," he said, maneuvering her to the tarp.

Her back settled into pockets of liquid, bathing her, making their foundation slippery, stimulating.

Preamble aside, he ripped at her shirt, then divested her of her panties within a jagged heartbeat. Juice pumped from her as he paused, looking into her eyes.

Looking *in* her, not *at* her.

The moment was terrifying and beautiful, and Tam didn't know whether to hide behind her usual wall of clothing or joking or whatever facade was available.

But…he was making her want to stay in the open.

"Dammit," he said, squeezing his eyes shut, then leaving her for a second. "Pain in the—"

It didn't take him long to fumble through his jeans and wallet, and when he came back she was opening her arms for him, dragging him to her over the slick tarp.

He made quick work of the condom wrapping, then

tugged on the latex. Even so, Tam could barely wait that long.

She flared upward, wrenching him down to her until he drove inside. Arching up to meet him fully, she jammed her hips against his, rocking against him in fierce time.

Her shirt was open on one side, baring her breast from where he'd torn at it. Her skin rubbed against his—wet, sliding, sticky.

She felt as light as fumes from the wine. The heat of their movements forced her upward, out of her body, out of her mind, as the pressure built.

Open...she needed to open up and—

He pounded into her, their bodies splashing on the tarp in a frenzy.

Something insistent pushed at her from the inside out, pushed, kicked, built...

Open...open up...

Then with a whoosh, she screamed apart. Sparks winged out from her into the air, then slowly fluttered back down, covering her skin with tingling sweat.

Soon Kyle came, too, collapsing on her, wine mingling with perspiration and her own lubricant as he pulled out.

His penis rested against her thigh as he kissed her neck, her jaw, his breath coming in gasps.

"Kyle," she panted, holding him to her.

His body tensed, and he buried his face at her shoulder. She thought that maybe she heard him curse.

Had she said something wrong?

Or was he already regretting what had happened?

As Tam wondered, she loosened her grip on him, giving him the freedom to leave.

Because that had been the deal in the first place.

No matter how much she wanted him to stay.

THE SOUND OF KYLE'S NAME slapped away Murphy's afterglow.

Everything had been going so well that he had forgotten himself. The old Murphy hadn't existed for as long as he'd breathed her in. For as long as he'd been a part of her.

It occurred to him that he hadn't been this happy in years. Not with work. Not with any other woman. Yet, just because he wanted to hold on to Tam all night, that didn't mean anything, right? Wasn't that what afterglow was all about, basking and wanting more? He'd get over this urgent craving to keep her. He had to. Hearing her say Kyle's name only proved it.

Dammit, he wanted to come clean. But doing that would only open a whole can of worms that his honesty wouldn't necessarily make up for. How would she feel if she found out Kyle had dumped her because she was "average Josie"? He wouldn't wish that on anyone, especially Tam.

And he would shield her from it any way he could. It was just too bad that the person he was protecting her from was now Murphy himself.

Murphy the bore, he thought. Hardly an item on Tam's wish list.

With a start he realized that this was maybe even a bigger issue—protecting himself from *her* rejection.

Not knowing what to do, he went with instinct, raising his head and tightening his arms around her. When words escaped him, he kept his peace, merely lavishing a gaze on her, tacitly apologizing for everything he'd done.

But she misinterpreted it. A hopeful smile lit over her, and his chest just about cracked in two.

"You know what?" Her forehead furrowed a little. "Nobody's ever looked at me the way you do." Then she added softly, "In fact, people don't really look at *me* at all. It's like they can't get past my clothes to see my face."

Sad, he thought, mainly because of what people were missing. There was a world of intrigue just in her gaze, a universe of interesting days in her smile. And that was only a start.

"Their loss," he said, meaning it.

At that she parted her lips, on the cusp of saying something else.

He just wasn't sure he wanted to hear what came next in a situation that was quickly becoming less and less of the game he'd first entered.

10

Kyle was watching her with such wariness that Tam rethought what she was going to say.

Wanting to keep him here, not drive him away, she chickened out and put on a smile instead. "So, I guess this is where we hang out, revel in the afterglow and all that?"

What she'd been intending to put out there, after revealing way too much emotion for her own good, was, *That was great, but I understand if you have to go, now that we're done with the fun. Really. It's cool.*

She'd wanted to give him an easy out, introducing the rejection first before he got around to it. But she actually liked having him here way too much to remind him of their initial agreement.

Besides, avoidance was much easier than having to deal with the aftermath of sex—especially this time. Something had been different from the wham-bam fun of the other night. Something that scared her.

At her return to outer lightness, Kyle looked relieved. Maybe she'd just been overreacting to the way his body had tensed—as if ready for running— after she'd uttered his name.

Optimism nudged at her. Was it possible he hadn't

had his fill of her? Was he actually going to stay, at least a bit longer?

While gauging her, Kyle leaned on an elbow, getting comfortable. Tam wanted to give a squeak of joy.

He wasn't going anywhere.

"You make it sound as though you're new to afterglows or something," he said.

Her skin was sticky, still alive with the impressions of his hands, his weight, a climax like a thousand cells crashing into each other. "I've had a few before, but…" She took in a breath; it shuddered in her lungs. "This was what you might call cataclysmic."

And she meant that—too emphatically. Jeez, what had she gotten herself into?

"Yeah?" An endearingly proud smile settled on his mouth. Then he nodded. "Yeah, it was."

Touched by hope, she ran her fingertips over his curved mouth, then down over his jaw.

The same random order of music played on in the background, as if nothing had changed from the start of the CD to the here and now. But a lot *had* changed, Tam thought. And as her mind began to work properly again, she realized just how much.

While Kyle watched her, she bit her lip to keep herself calm. To keep herself from saying something that had no business butting into this idyll.

I could fall for a man like you.

Rattled, her brain started racing. Maybe they should end this thing before it got ugly, before she was mugged by disappointment, before her feelings had more of a chance to grow.

Kyle's brows had drawn together, as if he was

holding back whatever was on his mind. But after a moment, something seemed to break free in his gaze, urging him on. "You okay?"

She tried to play it off. "Sure."

"Because you look sort of…" He searched for a description.

Tam decided to be only a tad honest. She didn't want him to think he'd done anything wrong when he'd done so damned many things right.

"I'm just thinking about…well, fate, I suppose. If we were different types of people…"

"Ahh." He got serious. "Right. If I were, for instance, capable of an actual relationship, you mean?"

"And if I were looking for one at this point in my life…" She dipped her finger in a stream of wine that had pooled on the plastic.

The rest went unsaid.

We might have had a good thing.

Silently she traced her dripping finger down the center of his chest. She couldn't get enough of touching him.

After a beat, his killer grin reappeared, chasing away any heaviness between them.

Following his lead, she switched on her flippancy to full force: her best defense. "I'll give you this, Kyle," she said, voice light. "You must've made a lot of girls happy along the way."

He just laughed. "But you're the only girl who counts right now."

"Oh, good answer. You always know what to say, don't you?"

"I've found that it's actually a natural talent." Clearly assuaged by her attempts at reintroducing some levity, he went with it, lying on his stomach, undoing the rest of her shirt, then sliding a hand to her hip. "But, best of all, I'm lucky. There're other guys you could've drawn from that vase."

"But you were the big winner."

They both smiled. He ran his hand from her hip to her breast, casually smoothing over it, as if admiring the shape, the gradual beading of her nipple.

As her skin hummed, she wondered so many things about him: when he'd gotten his first kiss, what girl he'd taken to the prom, how many times he'd had his heart broken, if at all.

"Just out of curiosity," she asked, "and, really, I'm only wondering—have you ever had a true girlfriend?"

Out of obvious avoidance, he lowered his mouth to her breast. With a defiant gleam in his gaze, he licked the circumference of it.

"Mmm, Bordeaux," he said. "My new favorite."

Groaning, she raised her hands over her head. "Okay, you don't have to answer."

"I'm getting to it."

He laved a nipple, taking his sweet time, bathing her with his tongue and sucking her to stimulation. She clutched at the tarp as he nibbled between her breasts, then broke away, shifting upward while gliding his sticky length along hers with maddening, sweaty friction. Resting on his elbow again, he came to wedge his thigh between her legs. As he moved it slightly back and forth, she felt her folds opening against his skin and kissing him with slickness.

Their casual, carnal position hammered at her from the inside out.

"I'd say," he finally whispered, "that I've never really had a relationship to take home to the family."

"A pot-roast kind of relationship," she added as her heartbeat threaded through her breathing, "where you've morphed into a couple instead of remaining two distinct individuals."

"That'd drive you crazy, wouldn't it? Not being your own person."

Subtly he moved his thigh, and she shifted her hips with him, coating him with damp evidence of her arousal. Her clitoris was stiff, hard against his skin.

"Well, don't *you* have me all figured out," she said.

"Not hardly."

He waited, as if expecting her to answer the same question about ever having a real relationship.

"I'm the same as you, Kyle," she said, giving in. Against his provocative movements, she closed her eyes, internalizing the sweet throb of her body. "No strings attached. You get like that when you've been dumped too much, right?"

He stopped teasing Tam with his thigh, causing her to open her eyes.

Sympathy. It was in his gaze again, just like last night.

"You know it's true," she said, acting as if it didn't bother her. "You know that after so many times, you stop caring. And you don't even entertain thoughts of anything long-term, because any feelings either one of you might think you have will always burn out."

They both stared at each other, and she realized that she hadn't come off so flippantly after all. Had she been opening some kind of door for him to go through? Had she slyly been inviting him to say that *he* wasn't that kind of man and that he, consequently, wanted to pursue something with her?

Bad idea.

His thigh remained where it was, against her, but he seemed distanced, conflicted in some way. And who could blame him with the trap she'd just sprung?

"Sorry," she said, doubling her efforts to be the blithe girl he'd signed up for. She adopted a voice that would fit the impression, one that would hide her simmering hurt. "I'm jaded. My parents got divorced when I was little. Ugly."

"What, do you think it'll happen to you, too?"

"I see it happening everywhere." She forced a laugh to cushion the words and pulled away from him. She sat up and hugged herself, pulling her shirt around her, closing her legs. She almost had her back to him. "The stories aren't the same, but the outcome is."

"What happened, Tam?"

Now that she'd started, she couldn't stop. He seemed so understanding, like a sounding board that would never tell her how wrong she was. Kyle was like her—he would get it.

"Just your basic tale of cheating and heartbreak." She hugged herself even tighter, but kept that I'm-over-the-pain smile on. Heaven help her if she lost it. "My mom screwed a guy at work, lied about it for months, and when my dad found out, she agreed to leave the house. Just like that—gone." She shrugged, forgot the smile, but still kept herself unemotional, even if she was the opposite, deep down. "My theory is that she was too ashamed to stick around because she all of a sudden got this overdeveloped sense of wrongdoing, and every time she looked at me or my dad, she'd relive her mistakes. To make a long story short, she moved out of state, left us because she thought it was noble or something like that, got remarried and never bothered to try to redeem herself."

"Sorry to hear that," he said gently.

"Doesn't end there. Even if my dad never talked about her, I know he was devastated. I never mentioned anything about the divorce to him, either, because I thought it would break him apart. It was like this ghost we knew lived with us but neither of us acknowledged it. And if he was a workaholic before the divorce— which is why my mom got lonely and cheated—he threw himself into his job even more. I guess he thought he owed me the best life, the best home. He wanted to make up for everything that'd happened."

"And instead of one house to live in, you got three." Kyle skimmed a hand down her arm, offering comfort.

"We went our own ways eventually—me to college, him to consulting jobs across the States." She wanted Kyle to keep touching her, keep drawing her out. The divorce had taught her to internalize and, now that she was with this man, all but bared of clothing and coverings, she realized how tired of it she was. Sure, she pretended to be so free—to not need anyone, but now, more than ever, she knew it wasn't working.

That he'd seen right through her.

All she wanted was to give up her shields, but it was hard, so hard, when all the world wanted to do was attack.

Kyle had gone on to stroking her hair, her strands

stiffened by drying wine. But he didn't seem to mind that, just as he didn't mind her face, her nose.

"There're people out there who can hold it together," he said softly. "People who never burn out on each other. My...aunt Bridget and uncle Gerald are an example."

Tam wanted to believe his fairy tale. But how could she when Kyle, himself, was an example of what she feared: a person who deserted you and then moved on to the next adventure? And here she was, having gravitated toward him. Warped.

"Happy endings?" she asked, not even bothering to mask her tone. "What about that cousin of yours. The workaholic?"

"What do you mean?"

At his stunned expression, she took his hand, kissed his knuckles, then said, "He sounds like a candidate for relationship burnout."

Just like her dad.

The obvious comparison knifed between them. She realized by his shocked posture how much this man must care for his cousin.

Well, now she'd done it, insulting his family *and* blabbing too much. Was Kyle ready to run now?

As the opera music faded to a stop, he flew against her expectations once again.

Getting to his feet, he held out a hand to her. After a pause, she locked her grip with his, and he pulled her to a stand. That same unreadable emotion she'd seen before had settled in his gaze.

"Where're we going?" she asked.

"The shower." He smiled, but it wasn't his normal

grin. No, oddly, this was a patient smile, the smile of a man who wanted more of her, even if it wasn't seduction and silk sheets.

But maybe she was projecting her own buried hopes onto him.

"And while we're in there," he added, "we'll talk about what we're going to do after work tomorrow."

She felt as if she'd been released from her own bonds of doubt. Impetuously she went to him, kissed him senseless, all the while knowing—and telling herself she didn't mind—that he'd extended their fling just one more day out of respect for the story she'd just told.

And that would probably be the end of it.

ON FRIDAY Tam and Danica were at their usual deli table, eating salads for lunch and watching the world go by from the floor-to-ceiling window. Her friend had just gotten back from an out-of-town business trip, where her team had used Tam's numbers as just a small part of their successful presentation.

"So, what's been going on?" Danica asked, twirling her plastic fork in the noodles of her Thai salad. "You haven't been giving me those nightly phone updates, so I have no idea what you've been doing."

Eyes burning from this week's lack of rest, Tam blinked at her friend. Danica looked as polished and cute as a button, as always, her dark pageboy perfectly coiffed, her cocoa skin smooth, her casual-Friday jeans and ruffled blouse all in order. But her brown eyes weren't as lively, her smile as dazzling. Now that Tam thought of it, even Danica's question held a slight tension.

What *was* going on?

"I'm up to the same high jinks," Tam said, flushed from the mere memories. "Kyle's been keeping me busy."

"Seriously? He's been over every night this week?"

Tam just nodded, smiling like a fool.

"You sex kitten!"

The conversations around their table seemed to come to a halt. Laughing, Tam shrugged at the eavesdroppers then bent closer to Danica. "A little louder? Mars didn't hear."

Hand over mouth to stifle her mirth, Danica lowered her voice. "Sorry, I'm just excited. When one of the Sisters succeeds, I get kind of crazy."

Then her eyes shadowed a little, and Tam didn't know what to make of the change.

"Don't get too stoked," Tam said, giving her friend a puzzled look. "It's still just a thang."

"Oh?"

Oh. She and Kyle had fallen into some kind of post-midnight habit, despite the fact that she'd truly believed he'd intended to extend their fling for only one more night. Still, she didn't expect anything to last beyond next week. After her spillage about her parents' divorce earlier in the week, they'd kept the conversation to small talk, tiny personal details that didn't reveal too much except a taste for mutually appreciated fun.

How far could you go on that?

Burnout, she thought. Inevitable.

Yet, she couldn't lie to herself anymore. The woman in her who secretly wanted affection, even if she knew it wouldn't last, was bothered by being just bed mates and nothing else. More than she would say out loud.

"Life works funny," Tam said, stabbing lettuce with her fork. "Kyle's the only man who's ever…well, gotten me, I suppose."

"Just too bad the boy's not in it for the long haul." Danica put her napkin next to her half-eaten salad. She seemed happy for Tam, but…what *was* it?

She was going to find out. "Okay, enough about me. Have you decided where you're going on your date tonight?"

A new business-card man for Danica. A new attempt at finding that elusive good time.

Her friend didn't look as enthused as Tam would've guessed she'd be. Jeez, what was it about everyone lately? Kyle was always surprising her by going against her expectations. And now Danica was doing the same thing.

"It's Chez Fleur tonight," the other woman said, starting to tear her napkin into strips around the edges. "Meet at the bar, have a few drinks to see if we should go on to dinner. The usual deal. I just hope this date doesn't suck as badly as old Dana from last week. I can't handle another night of strenuous chiding about my stance on politics, etcetera. Ugh."

"This one's bound to go better."

"Coming from a girl who just walked into The Boot meeting and picked out *the* card on the first try?" Danica shredded another part of the napkin.

Ah, so that's what this was about.

"Danica?" Tam put her hand over her friend's. This was the woman who'd welcomed her to the office and the city with open arms. "Something good's going to happen for you."

"I… Oh, boy. Now I've done it." She laughed uncomfortably. "Listen to me. I sound like a jealous harpy because you hit it out of the park during your first time at bat, and I'm whiffing with every swing."

"You're frustrated."

"Damned straight, but I'm also really happy for you." She held tighter to Tam's hand. "But…all right, I'm just going to come out with it. Tell me you're not going to be one of those women who ignores her friends because she's spending every free moment with her new man. I mean, it's great that you can, but I hope you don't become a capital-*G* girlfriend."

Stunned, Tam blinked. She hadn't seen that coming, and it was the last thing she wanted: to become a couple instead of remaining an individual, to be eaten up by some entity that robbed her of her own identity. She'd feared that an office job would do this to her, but she hadn't stopped to think the same thing might be happening with Kyle. She thought she'd taken precautions against that.

Tam braced herself for the sky to fall at the loss of her freedom…but nothing changed. Nope. Muzak still played on the deli's sound system. The rat race still continued outside the window.

The only thing that had altered was—whoa, it was true, now that she thought about it—her perception of how much Kyle might actually complement her, not rob her of everything that made her distinct and interesting.

Tam squeezed her friend's hand. "I don't want to be that type of person, either, Dan. So…" She nodded in determination. "Tomorrow night. We'll go out to dinner, because men like Kyle, who are just flings, don't take girls out, and I miss it." Even if he *did* make her the most exquisite meals. "And then we'll go dancing. Or to a movie."

"You don't have to give up a night with Kyle for me. I'm just making a point."

"I *want* to spend time with you." Especially since they were just getting to be good friends.

And friends could last much longer than someone like Kyle would.

Even if she wanted more from him.

LATE THE NEXT NIGHT at Shaw O'Grady's, the real Kyle was enjoying a Guinness while an Irish quartet performed in the corner on a squeezebox, guitars and percussion. All the patrons were tapping their feet on the plank floor and singing along to folk tunes while a few people reeled around in a beer-soaked dance.

As with last weekend, a bunch of celebrating college girls had claimed the table behind Kyle, and he had strategically kept his position at the bar in front of them. He was only waiting until their Saturday-night giggles turned into invitations.

In the meantime he drowned his sorrows—if that's what you called them. Maybe they were more like pokes at his conscience that'd been enflamed by Tuesday night's dinner.

Typical Sullivan feast. Murphy had been the soaring bird of success while Kyle had been the statue that bird had pooped on. And as more beer slipped down his throat, he was realizing just why that was, too: he'd never done much to earn respect, so why did he deserve it?

How would it feel to have Aunt Bridget and Uncle

Gerald applaud him for even one exceptional achieve-
ment? It wasn't that he had any doubts about their love,
not at all; they'd given him and his sisters a good home
and raised them like their own after Kyle's parents had
died young. It's just that Murphy, the brains of the
family, was heading down the path of success and
money. Kyle had never put himself in the position to be
questioned the way Murphy was, concerning the bar
exam or his business future.

What got to Kyle even more about the dinner,
though, was the way Murphy had cooled off toward
him. In the kitchen his cousin had barely even talked to
him.

But Kyle knew why. The way he'd been last weekend
with the blind date had been the final straw for
Murphy's tolerance of Kyle's antics.

And, as much as he hated to acknowledge it, last
weekend had also triggered Kyle's self-awareness.

How could he change anything, though? All Kyle knew
was that he didn't want to suffer under Murphy's disappointed gaze anymore. Nothing was worth that price.

Thomas, the bartender, strolled over, wiping the bar
with his cloth. "You stakin' out your territory for the
night, here?" he yelled over the music and caterwaul-
ing.

In a blip of even more awareness, Kyle realized that
too many of his conversations with others took place in
rooms where yelling over music was necessary. Man,
that was sad.

In answer, Kyle nodded, and Thomas went on to
another customer. Yelling just didn't seem all that appealing anymore.

Unable to help it, he went back to thinking about what he'd done to earn such outsider status with his cousin and what he could do to change that. Crap, what he'd give to relive that night with the blind date and change Murphy's mind about him.

The date… What had been her name?

He could check his phone. Even though he'd scribbled down her home and cell digits on a now-forgotten piece of scratch paper that was buried beneath all the junk in his apartment, he'd taken care to enter the cell number into his own mobile phone right away, in case he needed to get hold of her for the date itself.

He got out his phone and accessed the memory.

Cindy? Jackie? No, it hadn't been a cheerleader name. Down, down…

Peggy, Susie…?

Tamara.

Kyle thought for a moment. And her last name started with a *C*. Damn, he couldn't remember it.

But at least he had her first name. Murphy might give him points for that. Maybe.

Then it hit Kyle.

Last weekend…if he could do it over again…

He could.

With one call to Tamara C., he could apologize to her for having Murphy show up instead of the actual Kyle Sullivan. He could make this up to her, and maybe Murphy would realize he was serious about getting back in his good graces.

See, already he felt a bit better. He could show Murphy—and himself—that he could respect women and date for more solid reasons than just wanting a pretty face to adore for a night. Maybe Kyle would even run the notion by Murphy first, just to see how he reacted and to save himself the trouble if his cousin thought he was just being ridiculous.

But, dammit, *no*. He wasn't going to back out of his quest to be a better man. He absolutely wanted to call this woman. She deserved an explanation for what he'd done. Kyle really did owe it to her…as well as every other girl he'd heedlessly dumped.

But was it a good idea? A whole week had gone by, and he might've already missed his window of opportunity.

"Hey, guy at the bar!" came the inevitable call of the wild from the table behind him.

The college girls.

It stunned him to realize he wasn't in the mood for this.

Nonetheless, he turned around in his chair, nodding to them. They all giggled at what they'd reeled in.

"What's your name?" said a brunette with a glitter rainbow on her tight shirt.

The others just laughed behind their foo-foo drinks.

When Kyle didn't yell out his name, the brunette hopped off her stool and just about skipped over to him, the smell of piña colada and powdery perfume overwhelming him. "You are cu-ute!"

How he'd ever enjoyed come-ons like this was a mystery to him, now that he and his Guinness had thought about it.

But when Kyle glanced back at her, she seemed to be reconsidering him, too.

"Cute," she said again, "but you're totally too old."

He really *was* done with this scene.

11

TAM. MURPHY WAS TRYING to get his mind off her as he and Kyle went one-on-one at the neighborhood school-yard's basketball court before Sunday brunch. Their game was a weekend ritual, a way to keep in shape and to let out the demons of the workweek.

But Murphy needed it for more than just that right now.

He dribbled the ball, his back to Kyle as his cousin tried to bar him from approaching the basket. Yet, despite every effort to keep his mind on strategy, it was impossible.

With every thump of the ball, his conscience nailed him.

Thump. You've spent too much time with Tam for her to be just a daredevil caper now.

Thump. So the only thing you can depend on to save your ass from telling her the truth is relationship burnout.

Thump. When she gets tired of you.

Thump. Because you're sure not getting tired of her.

Out of pure frustration with himself, Murphy broke for the basket, slamming into Kyle, shooting.

And missing.

"Where's your game?" Kyle asked, taking the ball

behind the baseline so he could start his own scoring drive. He wasn't mocking Murphy; in fact, he seemed concerned.

Sweating and panting, Murphy backed up, on the ready, until his cousin was ready to take him on again. But even in the few seconds that he waited for Kyle to reenter the court, a slew of thoughts deluged him.

What're you going to do about her? his conscience prodded. *What're you going to do about* you?

Murphy's chest caved into itself at the answer: if he wanted to keep seeing Tam, he was going to have to find a way to tell her about his deception.

But how? How would it all make sense without him including his initial motivation—saving her from finding out that Kyle had dropped her because of the way she looked?

And…God, then there was his wild-man persona, something he knew he would have to ditch whether he wanted to or not….

Yeah, right. I'm not going anywhere.

It was the voice of the daredevil. A guest who'd settled in and stayed so long that he'd become a de facto part of the family.

Of Murphy.

God, it was true. Somewhere along the way he'd absorbed the change, and the fit was even more natural than the constricting suit of the please-everyone man. He was a bit of both, responsible and mature, but also relaxed and willing to engage in what he used to think of as decadent.

With a start, he realized that being with Tam had shown him that he wasn't so much wearing a mask *now* as much as he had been wearing one *before* in order to make everybody around him happy.

Still, the bottom line was this: if he told her who he was, the best part about finding himself would be taken away. She'd already cast judgment on him the other night, predicting that "his cousin" would end up like her dad. What would she think if she knew he was that guy, albeit one who'd altered because of her? Would she be able to change her mind about him, the drone doomed to break a woman's heart?

Her heart?

Any woman would be nuts to get into a relationship with the man she obviously thought "his cousin" was.

Across the blacktop, Kyle started to lean forward in slow-motion readiness to enter the court. Murphy kept eye contact, body tensed to defend, brain still going a hundred miles an hour.

But it hitched on one painful element: Tam's divorce story, a tale that had tortured him with the realization that she'd been hurt enough before and he was only adding to that with his games.

Jerk, jerk, jerk, his conscience repeated.

With a blast of energy, Kyle darted forward, but Murphy was still immersed in his fog. As a result his cousin made an easy lay-up, earning him two points.

Darting him a baffled glance—Murphy never got trounced like this—Kyle passed him the ball so they could set up again.

Murphy took his time getting there, gripping the ball in one hand.

"Murph!" Kyle was jogging up and down on the blacktop to keep his winning mojo going. "You turned zombie on me? You're playing like you stayed out all night or something."

"Back off, Kyle."

Unthinkingly Murphy stuck the ball under his arm. Even though Tam had gone out with her friend Danica last night, she'd still asked Murphy to come over after he'd finished bartending. And he'd done it, too—no hesitation, no second thoughts. In fact, he hadn't hesitated *any* night this week.

Hell, how had he filled his time before he'd met her? Work. That was the answer. Excuses and meaningless papers that could've waited for another day.

"You wusses takin' a tea break?" asked a loud, gravelly voice from the sidelines.

Both Sullivan boys turned to see their cousin Ian, Murphy's boss at the firm. He had graying, flyaway hair, red circles around his eyes and a donut-diet belly. Dressed in a Hawaiian shirt and Birkenstocks, he clutched a shoulder bag full of legal briefs since he never went anywhere without his work. As the topper, an unlit cigarette hung out of his mouth, moving every time he spoke.

My future, Murphy thought. *I'll be Ian in twenty years if I don't do something about it.*

Unsettled, he said, "Just in time for brunch, Ian. Mom's going to be beside herself with joy."

"Then that makes two of us," the older man said dryly. He flicked a lighter to his cigarette, coughed, then seemed to enjoy the hell out of it.

"Ian," Kyle said, "why don't you take the ball from your apprentice and shoot a few hoops with me."

Apprentice. Murphy felt trapped at the description.

"You think *I'm* a gamer?" Ian asked, ciggie bobbing. "Son, I'm just here to poke fun at the two of you amateurs. Then I'm going to eat until I bust a gut and listen to Bridget henpeck me because I don't visit enough."

Murphy bounced the ball, capturing his cousin's attention. Immediately Kyle got back into competition mode, face lighting up at Murphy's revitalization.

As if trying to break from the "apprentice" label, Murphy charged into the court, decimating his opponent's block and going in for his own successful lay-up.

"You just got a mud facial, Kyle," Ian, the peanut gallery, called from across the yard.

Kyle ignored their relative. "*Now* your tail's on fire, Murph?"

"I finally got warmed up."

"I'll say."

There was a note of the usual admiration in Kyle's tone. Obviously, his cousin was trying hard to tone down the competitive cracks and taunts today. Come to think of it, Kyle had spent the past week mellowing out, and Murphy wondered if the previous weekend's argument had anything to do with that.

But Kyle's obvious atonement emphasized Murphy's recent hypocrisy, and that stung. Still, Murphy wanted to be proud of his cousin; he indeed hoped Kyle had been thinking hard about what'd happened with Tam.

Just as hard as Murphy himself had been thinking.

He maneuvered the ball away from Kyle as his cousin reached for it. "So…I haven't gotten to ask. How're things going?" That was his way of wondering if Kyle wanted to talk about it.

Kyle seemed taken aback. "Good. I guess. Why?"

"I don't know, you just…this past week…"

Kyle put his hands on his hips, staring at the blacktop. "I've been meaning to talk to you about that."

Thank God. Enough of this tension between them. Enough of Mom's constant hints about how blood was thicker than water and how cousins should appreciate each other.

Posture lacking the regular confidence, Kyle continued. "What would you think if I called Tamara, from the blind date? I mean, to make everything up to her?"

Murphy's world flipped upside down.

Kyle…Tam…together…

Hell, no.

At what must've been Murphy's flabbergasted gaze, Kyle got sheepish, probably thinking Murphy was about to rip him yet again for proposing such an odd idea about the girl he'd dumped so unceremoniously.

But they were interrupted by the peanut gallery.

"Yo," called Ian. "You two run outta gas? Entertain me!"

Murphy held up a hand to him; it was something he never would've done to his boss in the office, but he didn't care anymore. "You want to call Tamara Clarkson?"

He snapped his fingers. *"Clarkson."*

"Do you even know her last name?"

"I do now." Clearing his throat, he shot Murphy a lowered glance. "And, yeah, I do want to call her. I've been rethinking the way I acted, and you were right, Murph. I was a shit."

Murphy realized just how much their confrontation had hurt Kyle. But…well, good for him. It was about time something got through that thick head of his and taught him how his insensitivity could affect others. They were both learning.

But, hell, why did Kyle have to grow a conscience now, of all times?

"Seriously—" Murphy tried to laugh, to keep calm, to disguise how horrified he was "—you don't have to do this to clear the road with me."

"Why do you think it's about that and not about her?"

Good question, but Murphy had his evidence. "You gave some pretty good explanations back at that lounge, Kyle. Remember when you said that you weren't attracted to her? Why would you want to mess with her now if you aren't really interested?"

At Murphy's intense tone, Kyle shifted his feet, put in his place. Murphy felt bad, but he couldn't allow Kyle to get in touch with Tam. No way.

"Listen," he added, "you've never had a problem meeting girls, so why don't you just be extra nice to the next one—"

"It's not about that at all. I regret what I did to Tamara."

Kyle's sincerity couldn't be questioned. Moved, Murphy unthinkingly put his hand on his cousin's shoulder. It was the first time he'd heard the younger guy say something so mature. Still, Murphy was fighting for his life here. "It's obvious you want to turn over a new leaf. You don't have to do anything to prove it. Okay?"

Say okay. Say okay....

His cousin glanced up, as if measuring the truth of

Murphy's sentiments. He didn't seem positive that Murphy wasn't still angry.

Boy, this wasn't going the way Murphy would've liked.

"Here's the thing." Heart in his throat, he pressed on. "Calling her and taking her out would be an empty gesture—not unless you really want to be with her. Do you?"

Kyle looked doubtful. Thank God.

Murphy was reaching, willing to do anything to keep this all from blowing up in his face. He would even lie to protect her—to protect what he had with her.

"And, truthfully, Kyle, she might not be all that open to the invitation. During our drink, she didn't seem too happy to have been stood up by you."

They'd never broached Murphy's drink with her before, so he could make up anything he wanted about it.

Saving the strongest argument for last, Murphy lowered the hatchet. "And Lord help you if you tell Tamara Clarkson why you left her sitting there. That's cruel."

"I thought I owed her the truth."

"Not if it does more damage for her than you."

Murphy was ready to choke with all the hypocrisy he was spouting.

But Kyle seemed to be considering these points. Had Murphy convinced him?

Come on, come on....

If you survive this, you've got to tell her everything when you go to her place after brunch, his conscience screeched. *No more putting this off.*

He imagined how devastated she would be when she found out. And he wanted to be there to divert the pain from herself and onto him, to take all the blame and anger, because he didn't want her to feel any of it.

That weird tingly feeling traced his heart again, but this time it grew stronger, until his emotions appeared clearly.

It wasn't that he was mourning the possible end to his Kyle masquerade. No, not at all, because he didn't *have* to give up this new freedom he'd found.

It was all about losing Tam.

As Murphy reeled under this thought, Kyle shifted, clearly uncomfortable with the open-ended conversation.

Through the haze of his realization, Murphy felt for his cousin, too. It'd taken a lot for him to offer up this act as an apology. It's something Murphy needed to imitate—like all the other Kyle qualities he'd been stealing.

He had to come out with the truth.

"You're good people, Kyle," he said, beginning to pat him on the shoulder but, instead, squeezing it in a bigger show of affection. "Just promise me you won't hurt her for the sake of misguided nobility, all right? I respect what you *want* to do. All the other women you meet from now on are going to benefit from that."

Fighting back a smile, Kyle shrugged, then went for the ball under Murphy's arm. As he stole it, then dribbled in place, he didn't even look at his cousin.

"It's hard having you hate me, Murph."

"I don't hate you. And, for the last time, forget calling."

Kyle didn't say anything, but his smile told Murphy that they'd come to an understanding.

Reaching out to cuff his cousin's hair in a rough return of sentiment, Murphy laughed, relief easing through his body until he felt ready to collapse.

It looked as if Kyle wasn't going to expose his disguise with Tam.

"About time you boys got it together," Ian muttered loudly from his perch on the sidelines.

Yeah, it was about time.

Now he just had to do the same with Tam.

AS THE LATE-AFTERNOON SUN blazed in the sky, Tam deserted her search through the job classifieds and answered Kyle's knock at the door. At the sight of him, her heart blasted awake inside her chest.

The weather had reddened his cheeks into patches of Irish-boy flush, and his arm muscles were straining with the weight of the packages.

"Got the works," he said, holding up the plastic bags full of ingredients he'd purchased for dinner.

"You spoil me." She took some of the burden, walking toward the kitchen as he shut the door behind him.

When he didn't answer, she turned around, finding a contemplative look on his face. What was up?

He caught her perusal, erased his frown and turned it into a grin.

"Believe me, you're worth every effort," he said, part charm and part…she wasn't sure what.

"Hmm. You seem sort of… Is everything okay?"

They placed the bags on the tiled kitchen island, under the hanging copper pots and pans. The room had come with a professional chef quality that Tam hadn't tampered with yet. But Kyle had made good use of it.

Just as she was about to ask him again if he was okay, Kyle reached out for her, took her in his arms and kissed her until she lost balance.

While his lips moved against hers, Tam's mind blanked out—just as it always did when he was around—taken over by soft white spaces where nothing existed except him.

Sighing, she returned his fervor, pressing against his hard body, molding herself until she forgot where he ended and she began. Instead of sapping her strength, every embrace only made her feel stronger. Last night at dinner, Danica had told her that the kind of quality guy who made women feel like that didn't make it into The Boot too often.

Tam imagined it was true. It's just that the whole affair stigma was making her wonder how to hold on when she should be letting go by now.

Speaking of Danica, well, maybe this was wicked of Tam, but she'd invited her friend to "drop by out of the blue" today to meet Kyle. They'd talked about him so much last night that Tam hadn't been able to stop herself. She wanted to show him off. But since she didn't want to freak him out and think she was getting all "girlfriend" on him, she was going to be a bit sneaky about it.

Hey, what was wrong with showing others what was so great about him? It didn't mean they were engaged or anything.

She leaned away from the kiss to gaze up at him while he toyed with her hair, as had become his habit. If she were a cat, she'd be purring by now.

"So what's on the menu tonight?" she asked.

"Besides you?"

She laughed at the innuendo, and he bent nearer again.

"Petite—" he kissed her forehead, as if unable to wait until he'd ended the phrase "—crabcake. Corn chowder—" another kiss, on her nose "—shrimp étouffée and a batch of—" he nipped at her mouth "—pralines."

If she weren't so daffy with lust right now, she would be tempted to tell him that it was strange how he lavished his time and talents on a passing thing like her. If anyone had walked into this room to see them hugging each other, they definitely might've mistaken them for a couple.

A *couple.* The word should've struck fear into her heart, but it didn't. Not right now, when it seemed so right.

With one final kiss, he pulled away and turned around to unload the bags. Although affectionate today, he really did seem extra quiet.

But Tam tried not to let the old doubts get to her. She was beyond that now, more confident about being wanted.

"Tam…" he began.

Oh, no. She didn't like the start of this. It sounded too much like the introduction of a serious conversation. And she knew Kyle didn't have those unless *she* ushered them in.

Absently she clutched her plain khaki skirt in both hands.

He took a breath and looked over his shoulder at her, his mouth partway open.

But when he caught sight of her, his gaze softened and he seemed to lose track of what he'd been about to say.

"God," he said, facing her all the way now, tilting his head as his gaze swept over her face. "I've never really told you how beautiful you are, have I?"

Her legs went wobbly, and she laughed a little, singed by the power of his tone. He almost sounded reverent, just like the night he'd been fascinated with her boots.

But they weren't having sex right now. No, it was just a quiet moment in a kitchen, a gap between heated encounters when he didn't have to be saying something like that to get her turned on.

Blushing furiously, her first instinct was to play down his compliment. She wasn't used to hearing that kind of sentiment, but right now it didn't seem so hard to accept.

"I've thought it a hundred times before, but…" Kyle shook his head, smiling.

"I know." Heartfelt comments weren't a common element of their repertoire. "Thank you, Kyle."

"Don't thank me." He trained his eyes on hers, but she couldn't read even a hint of what was in them. "There's a lot I need to tell you."

He was so intense that she actually backed against the kitchen's island. Oh, God. Had he just been buttering her up for the big boom? Was he going to put an end to their meetings right now?

Panic and denial raged through her. This couldn't be it.

In the other room, where she kept her purse, she heard her phone ringing. Danica? Was she warning Tam that she was about to arrive? After all, it was time for her to be here already.

But, really, Tam didn't care who it was. The call was an excuse. Any excuse not to hear what he was about to say.…

Throat stinging, she darted out of the kitchen for her phone.

But Kyle was on her tail.

As she made a grab for the call, he intercepted her,

holding the ringing instrument above his head so she couldn't get at it.

"Listen to me, Tam—"

"It might be an important call. Give it to me."

Stubborn as all get-out, he refused. "Just listen."

"Kyle!"

MURPHY FLINCHED at the name. He had to get this out in the open before he lost courage altogether. It seemed the most important thing in the world.

Compromising, he decided to let her check the number to see if the call was so important. He wouldn't give her the chance to break his momentum by ducking out unless it was urgent. He had an idea about why she was being so difficult anyway—maybe she thought he was breaking this off.

And maybe he unwillingly was. It all depended on her reaction.

"Here." He checked the phone's screen.

And saw the familiar number.

Kyle?

Dammit, what was he doing? He'd said he wouldn't be calling Tam. Or…wasn't that what he'd said?

What the hell was he going to do?

Trying to play it cool, Murphy summoned his new store of risk-taking talent and pressed the answer button. Just as quickly, he hung up, then kept the pressure on the button, turning off the phone. He knew that his cousin only had her cell number programmed in his own phone so at least Murphy was confident that he'd be able to tell her everything before Kyle could get back in touch.

Tam stared at him, mouth agape. When she recovered, she spread out her hands. "Why'd you do that?"

"It was an unknown number."

He felt as if he was being dragged down a drain. And at the bottom of that dark pit he was being sucked into, he saw Tam's shock and dismay at what he'd done to her. At what the real Kyle had said about her.

This was his best chance, but he just couldn't come out with it. The thought of her embarrassment shredded him.

But any way he sliced it, wasn't she going to hurt? She clearly was doing everything *she* could to avoid hearing him break up with her.

Dammit, dammit, dammit.

She'd gone silent, but as he slipped the phone into his pocket, she fisted her hands at her sides. "I suppose you want to say that all good things come to an end, huh?"

"Maybe they sometimes just change form."

Obviously confused, she shook her head, eyes narrowed as she tried to understand what he was getting at.

How was he going to *do* this?

His gut tied itself up with nerves. She was going to hate the real him.

Then something flashed into his mind: what if he'd missed the point here? He hadn't been Kyle the *entire* time he'd been with her, right? Bit by bit the real Murphy had emerged in her presence, and she'd seemed to like him. Murphy had been the one who'd dried the rain from her skin. Murphy had listened to the divorce story and tried to make her feel better about it. Murphy was the one who felt more strongly about her than any other woman he'd ever met.

In spite of all his worries, was Murphy really the one she would want to keep? Or did she want Kyle, the guy who would run out on her?

He braced himself, about to find out.

"I'm not the guy you think I am," he finally said.

She shook her head, narrowed her eyes even more, then ventured a tentative smile. "This is news?"

Huh? What was she saying? She already knew?

"I've told you before," she said, sounding more relieved by the second, "there're moments I think you're one person and then you surprise me by acting an entirely different way. But we're all like that. Nobody really knows everything about us, and we show different sides at different times."

Okay. This was a start, at least. "There's a reason I seem to have an abundance of conflicting personality traits."

"You don't have to tell me." She shrugged, blowing out a sigh and probably thinking that this was all there was to his confession. "You know I feel the same way about myself. Life is a progression of trying on different styles, jobs, even relationships to see what fits, don't you think?"

"Sure…but…" Ah, this wasn't getting any easier.

"Kyle, you scared me with all that intensity back in the kitchen."

A knock sounded at the door.

Comedy of errors, he thought. That's what this was. Except, he wasn't laughing.

Lickety-split, Tam was shooting toward the entry, flushed and energetic and probably really happy to be rid of this conversation. She was thinking he'd made a mountain out of a dunghill with all this not-the-guy-you-think-I-am existential talk. Brother.

She flung open the door.

"Hiiiii!" said a gaggle of female voices.

"Hi…everyone!" Tam sounded surprised as she disappeared over the threshold to hug whoever they were. Seconds later she tugged in a perky African-American woman by the hand.

Then two more women followed: a tall, lithe female who commanded the room, even with her Shirley Temple blond curls, and then a spiky-haired brunette wearing the most interesting zebra-print shoes. The blonde was carrying two plastic bags full of what mainly looked to be booze.

"Kyle, these are my friends—Danica, Pamela and Teena."

"Glad to meet you!" Danica said, waving at Murphy as he lifted a numb hand in greeting to the group. "We brought over some happy-hour ingredients."

Tam gave a polite laugh, glancing at Pamela and Teena. "This really is a surprise."

And as the women began telling them about how they'd just been to a matinee in the area and thought they'd stop by Tam's for a "bust in," he saw his opportunity for honesty whoosh by.

The only thing he could do without causing a scene and embarrassing Tam in front of her friends was summon his patience for a little longer and play the part of host.

But all the while he would feel Tam's dead phone weighing heavily in his pocket.

12

"So, Kyle," said Teena as she sat on the kitchen counter with her margarita. "Have any hobbies?"

As if taking pity on him due to all the damned questions the women had been launching for the past half hour, Tam turned on the blender, the blades giving him a slight reprieve with the whirring tequila, ice and strawberry mix.

Still, Teena, Pamela and Danica—a jury of single women—were all watching him, waiting out the noise for a response. They looked friendly enough, but Murphy couldn't help thinking that they'd come here for more than just an afternoon surprise party.

Back in the living room, he'd sidestepped innocent questions such as "What restaurant do you work at?" and "Do you have brothers or sisters?" and other personal tidbits Murphy had managed to avoid with Tam—who deserved the answers way more than her friends did. Because of their "understanding," Tam hadn't asked and he hadn't offered.

But he wasn't altogether happy with this arrangement, now that he'd gotten to know her more. Now that he wanted to know what made that smile of hers go from happy to thoughtful, what made her find it hard to get to sleep some nights and what made her burst out of bed in the mornings.

He knew her well enough to *guess* that her head was so filled with creative ideas that it was tough to settle down before midnight. And that she was anxious about getting to her job each morning so she could earn that paycheck and fund her idea of a perfect life. Yet these suppositions only brought up more questions and cranked up his fascination with this woman—a so-called free spirit who seemed to be not so entirely free at all sometimes.

But maybe he was just reading too much into Tam, filling in the blanks of what he didn't know.

At any rate, Murphy had quickly tired of the inquisition from her friends and casually gone to the fridge for a beer. Bad move, because they'd just followed him into the kitchen for the start of their impetuous cocktail party.

Now the blender stopped, opening Murphy back up for more.

Pamela, the obvious leader of the pack, was already on her second drink, but she didn't seem affected. Every blond ringlet was in place, every crease of her slacks crisp and perfect.

"You like sailing, surfing, jogging…?" she asked, continuing Teena's hobby question.

Just relax, he told himself. *Use that charm you've recently discovered and everything will be fine.*

"Wine tasting," he said, grinning. "I'm just discovering the joys of that."

Obviously caught off guard at the double meaning, Tam turned a laugh into a cough, then tried not to smile as she poured some margarita into a glass.

Like his evasive maneuvers in the living room, this one had been easy, as well.

He started to tap the beer bottle against the kitchen table. When would these women leave so he could be alone with Tam?

This was driving him nuts, sitting here and seeing his wristwatch blinking up at him with every second that passed. But at least with Tam's phone still in the off position in his pocket, the threat of Kyle's attempt to get hold of her was nullified. For now.

Murphy had to come clean before she asked for her phone—before she turned it on and listened to her voice mail, where Kyle would no doubt innocently reveal the truth.

God, he would feel a lot better if he could talk to Kyle right now and somehow tell him to knock off the phone calls.

He increased the tempo of his bottle tapping.

When Danica pursed her lips and gazed at his nervous gesture, Murphy stopped himself, then grinned in acknowledgment.

"Another round, girls?" Tam asked, raising the blender pitcher.

"Right here," Pamela said, holding out her half-empty glass.

At this most helpful distraction, Murphy got to his feet, intending to do *something* instead of just wait here in the hot seat. "I have a call to make. Don't mind me."

"Take your time," Danica said, dimpling at him.

"That's right," added Pamela, toasting him with her now-full glass. "We'll just be working our way to the worm."

Murphy glanced at the tequila bottle. There was a lot of booze left.

"You might have to graduate to some shots for that," he said, walking toward the door.

"Good idea." Teena almost fell off the counter when she grabbed for the bottle.

As Murphy left, Tam held the glass to her lips and winked at him. His chest warmed with a sensation he couldn't give a name to.

Puzzled, yet somehow wanting to cling to the soothing flow of this unexpected feeling, Murphy wandered outside to the stone steps leading to Tam's house. Even in late afternoon, the sky was getting dark because of a few grumbling clouds.

Murphy looked around, making sure he was alone, then took out his own phone and dialed Kyle's cell. He would have to convince his cousin to lay off without letting him know Murphy was with Tam.

If he'd learned any persuasive skills whatsoever during his education, now was the time to put them to good use. Forget going to trial—this was Murphy's judgment day.

The connection rang once, twice, then Kyle answered.

"Murph! What's up?"

Caller ID had identified him. "Just doing my thing."

"Paperwork. That's a hard guess."

"Hey," he continued, diving right into the crux of the situation. "I just need to make sure of something. That conversation we had before brunch—you weren't serious about it, were you?"

His cousin all of a sudden got real quiet—a kid who'd been caught jumping on the bed during naptime.

"Kyle?"

"Well…yeah." It wasn't hard to imagine Kyle looking all stubborn on the other end of the line. "I was definitely serious, Murph. In fact, I already tried calling, but I think her cell's off or on the blink. Who knows? But I left a message."

Murphy's heart jumped. Backed into a corner, on the edge of getting caught, the Kyle in him crouched in readiness, as eager for this challenge as he'd been the first night and at the masquerade.

But then he thought of Tam, and his heart dropped.

Suddenly there was no adrenaline. Just a lagging jab of regret taking the place of each pulse beat.

Murphy braced one leg on a higher step, leaned on his thigh and rubbed a hand over his face. "What did you say to her?"

"Nothing much." His cousin sounded encouraged, as if he was happy that Murphy had taken an interest in his quest for redemption. "I just reintroduced myself, apologized for not being able to make the date and told her that I hoped she'd let me take her out to make up for my absence. That's all."

That's all. Kyle had no clue what a disaster this was.

"And you're going to follow through?" Murphy asked.

"Of course. I meant it this morning when I said I wanted to do this. I was wrong to be such an ass to her. And I won't do or say anything to make her feel bad."

Murphy knew Kyle wasn't yanking his chain. He seemed genuinely sorry. God, he wanted to be glad for it, too, because if there was one thing that broke Murphy's heart the most, it was Kyle's potential to be so much more than a jerk.

Now it seemed he'd finally decided to turn a corner, and that filled him with great joy.

But it also made him angry that it'd happened during his journey around his *own* damned corner.

"I know you have a lot of interest in this, Murph, since you're the one who had to pick up the pieces after I left her there," Kyle added. "But don't worry. Your part is done. You won't have to come to her rescue again."

"How do I know that for sure?"

"Man, can't you just trust me on this?" Kyle sounded wounded. "I know I've spent a lot of time screwing up, but why can't you just give me a chance?"

He deserved one, Murphy thought. And he wanted so badly for Kyle to come out smelling like a rose, too.

If it were any other woman.

Instinct pressed him to tell Kyle what'd been going on, but Tam deserved to know first. And Murphy begrudgingly admitted that he was mortified about how Kyle might react. He didn't want to see the guy who'd been like a younger brother to him get that disappointed look on his face when he found out how Murphy had fallen from grace. How his role model had become such a hypocrite when it came to treating women with honesty.

The truth shook him. Murphy wanted to stay a hero in Kyle's eyes. He liked being looked up to, being the family golden boy, just as much as he liked his newer side.

He cleared his throat, hating the tightness strangling him. "You do deserve a chance, Kyle, and I'm going to help you in whatever way I can. I just—"

"You just don't think I should be diddling around with Tamara again," Kyle sighed roughly. "But that's the point. I'm not out to hurt her. I'm going to set things right."

"So you believe in karma now."

"I believe in showing you I can do it."

Kyle's bare admission startled Murphy. They'd never been so candid before. Maybe the screen of a phone call was all they'd needed to speak openly.

A breeze huffed at his back, and he glanced around, checking again to see that he was alone.

And he was. Very, very alone in this.

He didn't know what to say to his cousin anymore. *Good luck? Hope you win her over?*

"Thanks for checking in on me, Murph. Things are going to turn out great. Trust me."

"Just…" He was at a loss.

Yet Kyle didn't seem to mind, now that he'd gotten that weight off his chest. "I'll be good."

"You'd better be." Murphy's voice had come out gruffly, an unrestrained threat.

But Kyle had already hung up.

Hell, he thought, tucking the phone back into the opposite pocket from where he was keeping Tam's. At least he had her phone so he could control when she received Kyle's message.

Which meant he still had a chance to deal with this mess tonight before it got irreparably out of hand…if that hadn't happened already.

KYLE TOSSED HIS CELL on the bed. On the other side of the partition that separated his bedroom from the kitchen and sitting area in his studio apartment, Cousin Ian was loudly complaining about the 49ers as they played the Cowboys. Kyle stepped past the partition to join him.

Stuffed with Aunt Bridget's brunch food, he was propped on the couch, stomach out to there, his wiry hair sticking out from pulling at it, just like most Bay Area football fans were doing this season. Kyle wondered why Ian hadn't gone home after the feast to watch in isolation, since he was so immersed in the game that Kyle might as well not have existed.

Maybe Ian didn't want to go back to his empty condo?

Kyle glanced around his own place, wondering what was better about this one: white walls, no pictures, just some pieces of furniture topped by the modest TV. But then there was the kitchen: his favorite place in the world. Stocked with Emerilware and Le Creuset gadgets, the room was where he could experiment with food in the privacy of his own home. He was allowed to pretend he had some purpose there, even if all his big talk about owning a restaurant and bar one day was basic bull crap.

What else could it be with a guy like him. Right?

Then he thought about turning over that new leaf and wondered if maybe…

Pensive, he sat down to continue what he'd been doing before Murphy called: finding Tamara's home phone number somewhere in the flurry of scratch paper littering his apartment.

When the TV went mute, robbing the air of screaming fans and the nonstop talk of the announcers, Kyle glanced up.

Ian was pointing the remote at him as if he could manipulate Kyle with it. "Murphy giving you some grief?"

"Isn't that a big brother's job?" Sure, they weren't technically siblings, but it fit.

"He sticking his nose where it doesn't belong?"

"Man, I thought you were watching the game."

"I've always got my ears finely tuned to everything around me." He rested the remote on his stomach, which provided a decent, though rounded, table. "Hazard of my job."

Kyle didn't answer for a minute. Instead, he wondered if he should say anything about Murphy's overconcern with Tamara.

His cousin didn't usually get so tied up in Kyle's women. Live and let live—that's what Murphy's stance on Kyle's dating practices had been in the past. At least, that's what Kyle had thought.

But ever since Murphy had gone into that lounge and come out defending Tamara with such vinegar—even volunteering to have a drink with her—something had seemed off. Kyle hadn't thought much about it, but now that Ian had brought it up…

"Murph's on me about a blind date from last weekend." Quickly, Kyle gave Ian the short-attention-span version of events. "And now he doesn't want me to see her again."

Ian coughed with the gravel of a smoker who needs a cigarette, and the sound turned into a "Hmm."

"What, 'hmm'?"

"Murphy," Ian said. "I notice he's been…preoccupied lately. That's why I'm bringing him up. Not that he's slacking off at work or staring out the window or some such nonsense—no, it'd slay Murphy ever to underperform. He's always been a top-notch asset and always will be. I'm talking about…" Ian glanced at Kyle from out of the corner of his eye. "What am I trying to say?"

Kyle knew this trick. Columbo. According to Murphy, Ian the lawyer often used it to wheedle information out of a witness or fellow professional by acting like he didn't know squat when he actually did.

Sneaky bastard. It made Kyle think over what information he did have about his cousin. He envisioned Murphy smiling to himself at the bar while cleaning up, Murphy grinning like a moron while they made dinner together in the Sullivan kitchen.

"He really hasn't been all there, I suppose," Kyle said. "But it's my fault. We had a rift because of the whole blind-date debacle, but it's better now."

"How so? It sounded like you were defending yourself on the phone to him about something. The blind date?"

"Uh-huh."

"Well, how can 'it' be 'better' when you were on your toes like that?"

"I was just explaining myself, that's all." Kyle went back to looking through the scratch paper. "Murph seems to think I need to justify taking this woman out again."

"You said he had drinks with her."

"One drink. To cheer her up after I ditched her."

"So he got to know her—even for a short time."

"I suppose."

Ian laughed, the remote bouncing up and down on his belly.

Kyle was afraid to ask what was so funny, because gradually an answer was coming to him.

"Maybe," Ian said, "Murphy likes this girl."

Unbidden, Kyle's competitive streak flashed over his vision, summoned from years and years of trying to top Murphy.

He likes *her?* he thought. *Then let's go head-to-head and see who the better man is.*

But, oddly enough, the proposition tasted dull.

Maybe it was because Kyle sincerely wanted to accomplish something with his second chance. This wasn't only about Murphy—it was also about proving something to *himself,* growing up and growing out of a life that was seeming more and more pointless with every passing day.

"You think so?" Kyle asked. "Murphy and…Tamara?"

"He's got hormones, too."

Kyle almost said, "Not like mine, he doesn't," because he knew his cousin would never be ruled by baser instincts. Besides, in order for Murphy to pursue anything with Tamara, he would have had to continue lying about what Kyle had done—and Murphy wouldn't embarrass her by telling her the "average Josie" details—so Ian's theory wasn't possible. Also, Murphy would never go beyond whatever little white fib he told that excused Kyle from the date in the first place.

"I don't buy it," he said, scanning a torn receipt with some numbers on it.

"Just conjecture." Using the remote, which was still resting nicely on his belly, Ian turned the sound back on.

But Kyle's mind kept whirring as he sifted through the chicken scratch on the papers.

Murphy's just being careful because he doesn't want me to hurt this woman again, he decided, *and that's all there is to it.*

He came to a *Sports Illustrated* covered with scribbles and there, in the capital S, was Tamara's name.

And two numbers.

Satisfied, Kyle chose the one that had the "h" for "home" next to it and went to the other side of the partition to make his call.

WHEN KYLE CAME BACK INSIDE the house, Tam's stomach cartwheeled at the sight of him, and she literally had to grab the counter to keep her balance.

He'd just gone outside fifteen minutes ago, but it felt like light-years.

Even a tickle of curiosity couldn't rob her of the thrill she got from watching him enter her kitchen. It was as if she was so tuned in to him that she could feel the heat of his skin across the room.

Smoothly, he cocked his head at the living room, summoning her to join him, and she put down her margarita to follow as he headed there.

"Whipped," Teena said, slurring.

Danica wasn't too far behind Teena in the fiesta sweepstakes. "Definitely a victim of luuuuv."

The drawn-out word froze Tam. Love? How did love apply to—

Oh, God. It should've sounded more ridiculous, should've made Tam scoff at the mere notion.

But… She recalled the way Kyle listened to her, the way he knew just how to look at her and send her into a fit of…what?

Love? She'd never experienced it, so she had no idea what it felt like. Was it a possibility? And how dumb would she be to fall in love with a man who was a temporary thing?

Pamela, who'd graduated to tequila shots and didn't

seem any the worse for it, merely saluted Tam as she walked by. Still, her smile spoke volumes.

"Okay, that's it." Tam made a "stop going there" sign with her hand. "Every one of you is acting like you're seeing the emperor's new clothes when he's actually just buck naked."

Teena scrunched up her nose. "Come again?"

"You're seeing something that doesn't exist."

A sound of disbelief came from Danica, and she and Teena began laughing hysterically. Easy drunks.

"I'll handle this," Pamela said, finger in the air as she turned to her friends with a very serious mock frown.

Okay. So she *was* three sheets to the wind. Luckily, they'd all taken public transportation or Tam would be worried.

Shaking her head, she left, finding Kyle near the door while he restlessly combed a hand over his jaw. Again the room around him seemed to fade away as her heart turned itself inside out.

"You summoned?" she asked playfully.

He pulled out of whatever was consuming him, his eyes coming to focus on her. Neither of them spoke for a second. Tam couldn't. She physically, unexplainably couldn't.

"When are they leaving?" he asked softly.

She swallowed, wanting more than anything to be alone with him. But, dammit, that wouldn't be happening for a while because she'd accidentally mentioned what was on Kyle's menu tonight and they'd gotten excited about that and before Tam knew it, they were staying.

"Somehow, they got invited to dinner," she said. "By me."

At his pained look, she decided to lay it on the line. "I'm so sorry, this all just *happened*. I wanted Danica to meet you and she ended up bringing Teena and Pamela, too, because they were all hanging out earlier today, and then the drinking started and—"

"I want to have you all to myself, Tam." His voice was low, scratchy.

Before she could inhale from the effects of his words, he stepped forward and ran his knuckles over her stomach.

Ooof. It felt like her foundation had been blown away, leaving her suspended in air and coming to a slow crash.

Still, Friday's conversation with Danica haunted her.

Tell me you're not going to be one of those women who ignores her friends because she's spending every free moment with her new man.

An individual, she thought. *What happened to wanting that for yourself? And who will you turn to when Kyle is gone?*

"I can't kick them out," she said. "They're my friends."

And you could be one, too, Kyle, she thought. *You could even be more than that if...*

It would never happen.

Red was creeping up his throat. "Tam, dammit—"

"Three hours." That sounded doable. "They'll be out of here in three hours after I help you with dinner and we eat. I'll pay for their extra helpings if that's what—"

"Of course that's not what's bothering me. I don't want your friends here while I talk to you."

Anger encroached farther up his skin, his cheeks. But then he seemed to get ahold of himself. Almost absently, he put his hand on his pocket, then removed it. Something was in there, but she didn't stop to think about what it was.

"I need to get more food at the store, then," he said, already turning to the door.

"Kyle—"

She grabbed his shirt before he left, pulled him back toward her. She kissed him recklessly, thanking him for not pushing the issue, promising him great things to come because he'd been so patient today.

Clearly encouraged, Kyle scooped her against him, lips hard against hers as he ravished her mouth. His skin, rough with emerging stubble, was musky and tinged with that lime scent she loved.

That word again...*love.* But she didn't, couldn't...

He sucked her lower lip while disengaging, a long pull of sexy foreplay. She almost felt like hitting the floor, then sprinting over it to kick the girls out of the kitchen.

But she'd already set the next few hours into motion.

"Three hours," she whispered, already starting a mental countdown.

With a harsh exhalation, he checked his watch, pulled open the door and gave her a parting look that just about had her roping him back in.

"Tam? You still here?" yelled someone—Pamela?—from the kitchen.

"Sure am."

When she got her strength, she struggled back to her friends, feeling hooked in the direction Kyle had gone.

Enough with the dramatics, she told herself. *He'll be back, and in a few hours we'll be alone....*

She settled down with the girls, trying to relax, hearing their chatter but not absorbing it.

A short time later a phone rang and, without thinking, she looked around for her cell. But the ringer wasn't playing a Mozart tune—

Wait. *Her cell.*

Now she recalled that Kyle had put it in that pocket he'd skimmed over when they'd been by the door. In all the activity, she'd put that situation on the back burner.

Had he forgotten, too? She would have to remember to get it from him when he came back.

The phone rang again. It was her house unit.

"I'll be back in a second," she said to the lushes, leaving them in the midst of a dirty-joke marathon in which they were replacing any and all names with hers and Kyle's. Lovely.

She went to the phone in the living room and picked it up.

"Hello?"

"Tamara?" a familiar voice asked.

She broke into a smile, wondering why Kyle was using her full name.

13

"KYLE," SHE SAID TEASINGLY.

There was a beat of silence, then he laughed. "Ah, got it. Caller ID."

Actually, this decorative phone didn't have the feature. Not that she needed it.

She lowered her tone, her libido going wild at just the thought of him: the undeniable lure in his cloud-blue eyes before he'd left for the store. "I'd know your voice anywhere."

Again the phone line crackled with a nonresponse.

What kind of game was this? She smiled, eager for it. For *him*.

Just as his silence stretched her to the breaking point, his voice came back on. And, for some reason, he sounded hesitant. Odd, after the way he'd stormed out of here earlier.

"I was hoping…after what happened…" He laughed again, this time slightly discomfited. "Listen, I'm at a little café here on Hyde Street. It'd be great if you could meet me so I can explain my side of the story."

As if his weird tone wasn't enough, she also wasn't sure what he was talking about. Or was he referring to the anger he'd shown due to her friends' surprise appearance? They'd already hashed that out. Well, actually, they really hadn't, so maybe that *was* what he meant. Having failed earlier, he was pushing to get her alone again, so he could elaborate on whatever he'd been trying to tell her before Danica and company had shown up. That had to be it.

Warmth enveloped her as she burst into a smile. Like the true player he was, Kyle was resorting to creative tactics to get her all to himself, and her body loved the idea, even if she knew she should stay with her friends.

The devil. He hadn't intended to go to the grocery store at all. And he knew she would be a sucker for his game, even if there were times when she thought they'd gotten beyond them.

"So you finally decided you wanted to meet me in public?" she lightly taunted, thinking of all the times they'd spent indoors since first meeting each other.

"Uh, yeah." Kyle actually sounded embarrassed. "I'm really sorry about all that. But I'll make it up to you if you meet me."

Oh, nice insinuation. She just bet he'd make it up to her.

Yet she hadn't meant to wheedle an apology out of him; they'd agreed upon the parameters of their fling. A private affair, right? Even if they'd met in public at the lounge the first night, they'd hidden away by themselves ever since: in the shadows of that beatnik bar; at a masquerade where their faces had been hidden; in her home.

Secret lovers.

But now, driven by the cynical patterns of her past, she started to wonder if there was more to it. If he, the gorgeous babe, didn't want anyone he knew to see him with a less attractive woman than he probably dated on a regular basis.

I've never really told you how beautiful you are, have I?

His words sang in her mind, even though he'd said them hours ago. And the way he drank her in with his gaze...

Her neurotic fears couldn't be true. She knew in her heart that he thought she was attractive. Very much so.

But, then...why was she still wondering?

The line had gone quiet again, as if Kyle wasn't going to force her into meeting him, after all. Switching position with the phone against her other ear and opening her mouth to offer another comment, Tam found herself facing her friends, who were loitering around the kitchen entrance. They had their purses, ready to go.

How long had they been standing there?

Unsteadily, Danica made a hold-the-line motion.

"Kyle, just a sec. Looks like my friends are about to take off."

"All right."

She'd expected him to sound happy about that, but he instead sounded neutral. Strange, when he'd been so adamant about getting the girls out the door.

Tam placed a palm over the mouthpiece, smiling at them.

"We're goin' bar hoppin'," Teena said with a goofy grin. Her drawl was more pronounced with the liquor.

As Tam started to ask them why they weren't staying for Kyle's dinner, Pamela, as regal as ever, interrupted. It seemed that when drinking, she didn't slur, she overenunciated.

"It's okay," she said, as articulate as a local newscaster, "we just wanted to see your Boot man. And we have orders to report back to Julia, right, girls? She's on *another* date with her guy, but she's still feeling proprietary about Kyle, seeing as she was the one who recommended him."

Teena gave a thumbs-up for Kyle. "Julia's gonna be prouder than a mama bear."

And with the way Danica and Pamela were beaming, Tam guessed that they thought he had possibilities; he'd been charming and only aired his frustration about their presence privately. Besides, a man who was willing to cook dinner for friends couldn't fail to impress.

Danica pointed to the phone, made a go-on-with-your-talking gesture, then pulled Teena toward the door.

Pamela trailed, whispering, "Dinner this week?"

With verve, Tam nodded, still holding the phone.

As they left through the front door, Tam returned to Kyle.

"Sorry about that." Her smile turned hungry. "But they're gone now."

"Okay."

Where was the excitement?

Jeez, why did it feel so surreal talking to him right now? Where was that connection she thought they had?

"So can you meet me?" he added. "It's the Red Square Café."

She knew of it, a small place within walking distance.

"You don't want to come back here?" she asked, baffled.

There was that awkward pause again, punctuated by another uncomfortable laugh.

"I know we did some big talking during our first phone call, but I'd just like to have coffee with you right now. If you don't mind. I'll…explain. Okay, Tamara?"

Now it felt as if she wasn't even chatting with the man she knew. There was a lack of passion, a total absence of the chemistry they had face-to-face.

God, she longed to see him again. And frankly she was curious as to what he was up to at the café: if this would be another foreplay scenario, perhaps where they would make love in a back room…or they would tear off each other's clothes in an alcove near a crowded street.…

Skin prickling with memories of his touch, she told him she would be there within twenty minutes, grabbed a sweater and her purse, then dodged out of the house. As she traversed the hill toward Hyde Street, the air chuffed at her, cooled by the sky's dark clouds.

Soon, she came upon the café, where she found Kyle sitting outside, the details of him made fuzzy by the distance she was quickly closing. Heart blasting, she picked up her pace.

Situated amidst the potted plants and wrought-iron tables, he was wearing a leather jacket, holding a foam cup. Her pulse jittered, rocked by anticipation.

She walked faster, the sooner to get to him. Her heartbeat accelerated even more, expectancy jolting through her.

He smiled and got out of his chair.

His leather jacket. Had he been wearing it earlier? She'd never seen it before. And the red of his shirt…?

He crossed to the opposite side of the table, still smiling, and pulled out a chair for her. Tall, dark, handsome…but there was something off about him, something she couldn't quite…

When he turned back to her again, he grinned, gray-blue eyes friendly but hardly passionate.

Shock cracked through her chest. She stumbled, stopped, limbs freezing, her gut fisting.

The same, but different. This man was a little more wiry, his shoulders not as broad.…

"I'm so happy you came, Tamara," he said. "It was touch-and-go for a while. Your cell hung up on me for some reason, but I'm glad your home number worked."

His voice—an echo of Kyle's but…

Not the same. Not the same at all.

"Who *are* you?" she asked.

MURPHY ARRIVED BACK at Tam's with groceries in hand, but when he knocked at the front door, no one answered.

Nonplussed—the women were probably whooping it up and couldn't hear from the back of the house—he went around to the kitchen.

But there was no answer there, either.

And when he peered in the window, the room was empty.

He went for his cell, then realized that he still had hers in his other pocket. No matter. He would just call the house number.

He heard it ringing inside and…no answer.

What the hell?

Had they left the house for more booze? No, they would've called him at the store for that. Had they gone somewhere else for some reason?

If that were the case, Murphy couldn't imagine Tam

not leaving a note. And he couldn't check the garage to see if her car was there—no windows. Plus, she hated driving in the city and rarely took it out. That's part of the reason she rode the bus to work—that and her determination to help the environment.

With a curse Murphy leaned against the wall, setting the bags at his feet. It was his fault he couldn't contact Tam; if he hadn't snatched her cell, he would be a whole lot more enlightened about where she'd gone.

But his self-directed anger was nothing compared to the nervous tension gripping his body. Every instant he'd spent at that store had been torture. All he'd wanted to do was be with her, laying out the truth and hoping she'd forgive him. He dug his fingers into his palms to distract himself.

Dammit, he wasn't going to think of what would happen if she rejected him tonight. But how could she not? He was going to sound like such a prick, especially since he wasn't going to include the trigger for the whole charade—Kyle's harsh comments about her appearance.

But he had to do it that way. He had to take the chance that she was going to hate him, because he sure as hell wasn't going to allow her to think she was any less than she really was.

Murphy's stomach clenched. The thought of losing her drilled into him like a sharp needle.

He didn't even want to think about what his life would be like without her. She'd only been a part of his nights for a short time, but it had been an intense time.

Chaos, he thought. *If I lose her and everything she's shown me about myself, I won't know how to find myself again.*

As Murphy waited, reeling under the threat of withdrawal, the clouds gathered.

Bad weather was on its way.

AT THE CAFÉ Kyle had chosen because of its Russian Hill location—the area in which he knew Tamara lived from their first chat—he cocked his brow at her strange question.

"I'm Kyle Sullivan," he said, stunned, but still using his basic charming tone of voice in his crusade to win her over. "Who do you think I am?"

She just stood there, mouth agape, forehead furrowed.

All right. Today's phone conversation with her had been kooky enough. But this was the *Outer Limits,* here.

"So you finally decided you wanted to meet me in public?" she'd asked, taking him aback with her bluntness in referring to how he'd ditched her at the lounge. But Kyle had chalked that up to his deserving it. Yet minutes later, hot as you please, she'd invited him back to her place.

Confusing. And, to top that, he wasn't sure why she'd been talking to him like they were so familiar. Could it have been because of their first phone call, when they'd been up-front about what they'd wanted from each other?

By now she was shaking her head with just as much puzzlement as he was feeling.

"Is this some kind of joke?" she asked.

"Joke? No… Listen, all I wanted to do was apologize for our date."

Now that he saw her up close, he realized that he'd been off about her looks. Unlike that night, when she'd seemed to be a shrinking violet, today she possessed a self-assured walk that drew the eye, an inexplicable dignity that wasn't obvious or cosmetic. Her clothing wasn't as weird, either—her skirt, blouse and sweater were all simple, classy.

Kyle bolstered his courage. This meant he needed to come clean about his first impression of her, because he'd obviously been so wrong. A girl with this kind of confidence would just laugh off the "average Josie" thing, since it was so ridiculous, right? Besides, this was about telling the whole truth and taking it in the chops for being a jerk, and he couldn't accomplish that by holding back.

But he would get to the embarrassing details of what he'd said to Murphy about her later. Getting whacked across the face before he had a chance to really show her he was sorry wasn't the point of this, either.

He shrugged, noticing that she wasn't quite following him. "My cousin, Murphy, was more than happy to have that drink with you, but that doesn't excuse what I did."

"Murphy?" Now her eyes were wide. Very wide. "What are you talking about?"

"My cousin. The guy who bought you the drink?" Kyle went for a little levity. "He looks a lot like me, but not as handsome?"

He tried to laugh as his joke clunked. Okay, not funny.

And, when Tamara's skin went pale, Kyle was more addled than ever. He rushed to offer the chair to her.

"None of this is making sense," she said, sitting.

Kyle grew even more agitated. He remembered what Ian had said about how Murphy maybe liked Tamara.

Remembered how angry Murphy had been after coming out of that bar. Remembered his secret smiles and how distracted he'd been this past week.

Queasy with questions, Kyle plopped into his own seat.

Murphy? Had he done something Kyle didn't want to know about?

"You did have a drink with Murphy," he said, testing.

A long brown curl slapped Tamara over the face, but she ignored it. "I had…well, more than a drink with a guy I thought was Kyle…. And he wasn't…you?"

"More than one drink," he repeated, the harsh truth starting to eat at him.

Tam tried to swallow, but her throat had closed up. More than one drink. She thought of the dark courtyard of that beatnik bar, the masquerade, the wine she'd sipped from his skin. Her body was cold, warm, hot at the same time.

"We've been seeing each other ever since that night," she managed to say. "His name's…Murphy?"

It was an empty name to her. A stranger's name.

Kyle, who looked so much like…*Murphy,* seemed as if he was a boy who'd just found out that Batman robbed banks. "Yeah, Murphy. Murphy Sullivan."

Discombobulated with growing anger, she tried to think of any personal details that she knew about the man she'd been so intimate with, and they were pitifully few. So this was why he hadn't wanted to talk about himself. This was why she'd been allowed to wax on about her life without him offering much in return.

Fury burned hotter inside her. Kyle…no, Murphy— his name was *Murphy*—had betrayed her. No wonder they'd never shown their faces together in public except for that first night. He'd been keeping her a secret so he could get off on this ultimate game of his.

She'd thought of him as a player, before, but he was more of one than she could ever have guessed, damn him.

"He told me," she continued, voice shaking, "that he was a waiter."

"He's a bartender at the same restaurant I'm at." Kyle—the real one—rubbed a hand over his face. "I don't get this. Murphy's the most honest man I know. He's—" He choked off, hanging his head.

Clearly Murphy had hurt Kyle just as much as he had her.

Murphy. He'd glided his hands over her naked skin, kissed her mouth, her most private places.

Tam's body tingled with ire and bedraggled affection that she didn't want to feel. She'd allowed him to become a part of her, to see into her. And she'd wished for even more than that.

Tears welled in her eyes, but she refused to let them free. No. Now, more than ever, there was a reason to keep them inside. This…Murphy had deceived her, just as her mom had deceived her dad. But she wasn't going to lose herself in work and sorrow as he had. She'd spent her whole life expecting a moment like this.

And she'd prepared herself.

No problem. She could go back to what she'd always wanted. She would stand strong and alone, where no one could affect her.

That's what she'd always wanted anyway. To be free. And more than ever, there was a reason for it.

In spite of her wishes, a tear streaked down her face, but she cuffed it away before anyone could see.

Love? she thought. She'd been so wrong to even think of the emotion when it came to Murphy/Kyle. This pain couldn't be a part of it. So maybe she'd never even been close to feeling love.

Her heart seemed to sink further into her body, burying itself in numbness.

When Kyle looked up again, he seemed disappointed in his cousin, as if Murphy had let him down in some profound way.

"Murphy," he said, continuing where he'd left off, "is supposed to be the responsible one in the family. He works himself so hard that…hell, maybe he just lost his mind?"

Cousin. A hard worker.

Tam recalled the times Murphy/Kyle had talked about "his cousin" with such regret and concern. "Is Murphy a workaholic?"

"The worst. He's going to be a lawyer, so he's stuck in the firm during the day and works in a bar at night to pay off his debts."

So Murphy was that cousin—a second coming of her tragic, workaholic dad. A recipe for heartbreak.

Voice flat and emotionless—because that's how she needed it to be—Tam told Kyle almost all of it, and they came to the conclusion that Murphy must have just decided to become a different person for a while. It was their best—and only—guess as to how this could've happened.

"It's like he really was this wild man." She dug her nails into her palms, the only way to keep her emotions in check.

What part had she played in his fantasy life, if that's

indeed what he'd been creating? Had he only been pretending when he'd looked at her with such affection and appreciation?

Surely that couldn't have been a lie, she thought. It'd all seemed too real....

She drew her sweater around her. "He's good at games, you know. I'm not surprised he fooled everyone."

"I just can't believe this."

Darkness was encroaching, engulfing her in its bleak chill. She felt like a small, lone cloud swollen with sadness and rage.

"Out of all those cards in The Boot," she said, on the border of tears again, "I had to pick yours. His. Whoever's."

"Any guy would be lucky to be with you, Tamara," Kyle said, watching her with compassion, as if he could be apologetic enough to cover for his cousin, too.

Tam, she thought, hearing Murphy's voice say her name instead. *He calls me Tam.*

Still, the real Kyle's sentiments touched her, even if she couldn't bring herself to smile so he would know it. Any facial movement—any movement at all—was going to bring on the crying. And she wouldn't give Murphy the credit for having gotten to her. Not if she wanted to survive this.

But...dammit.

She wanted *her* Kyle back, but without all the doubts that had been gnawing away at their encounters. She wanted the man she thought he might be under all the games they'd been playing. She wanted the man who'd slowly brought out the woman who'd been hiding under the façade—the one with fears that he'd been able to quell, the one who felt so much better about herself now.

The tears were building again, but she fought them tooth and nail, determined not to let them rule her.

"Please don't cry," Kyle said.

"I won't." Her voice sounded as if it'd been dragged through shattered glass.

Making an attempt to gather herself, Tam met Kyle's gaze. He looked guilty. Why? This wasn't his fault.

"Listen, Tamara." His lips tightened, but then he got a resolute look on his face. "I need to apologize, too. I think I'm what might've gotten Murphy started on this…fiasco." He blew out a breath. "When I saw you in the bar, I made a snap judgment. It was shallow, I know that, but I decided you weren't the kind of woman I'm…well, *in* to. And he decided that instead of letting you know why I was leaving, he'd have a drink with you and make excuses about why I wasn't there. He didn't want you to know what I'd said."

Which was what? She didn't want to know, but neurotic possibilities bit at her, anyway. Fear of her unattractiveness, planted after the divorce when she'd wondered why she wasn't good enough for her mom, cultivated by boys who used her on one or two dates then ended up leaving, too.

Hadn't she been wondering why a guy like Kyle would even give her a second glance?

She waited for the mortification to come and swallow her whole.

But then she remembered the first moment she'd seen the man she'd believed to be her date in the lounge and recalled the way his eyes had lit up at seeing her.

That'd been *Murphy,* she realized, heart thudding. And he'd been attracted to her even then. She absolutely knew it.

"I was being a jerk," Kyle continued, spreading out his arms as if to offer himself up as a target. "I was wrong, because you really are pretty, up close, Tamara. I mean that. And I'm only telling you the truth because it's so damned obvious I was blind."

He seemed to be waiting for her to take a shot at him, to tell him that, yes, he was an A-1 moron.

But she couldn't. His confession seemed so trivial in light of everything else. "I appreciate that, Kyle. I really do."

Amidst the darkness, a tiny flicker of hope wavered to life. She was attractive—it wasn't hard to believe anymore. No one could tell her any differently, not even herself. Not after Murphy...

The real Kyle heaved out a breath, no doubt relieved and simultaneously burdened with what they'd discovered about his cousin.

She tried to take it all in: Murphy had wanted to protect her from Kyle's opinion, and that's how it'd all started. She clung to this, but how could she forgive Murphy for the rest of it that easily? He'd *lied* to her, just as her mom had lied to her dad.

What was she going to do? She wanted to give the man who'd affected her so strikingly a chance to explain. God, yes, she did. Maybe it was because she knew in her soul that he really was good for her because he'd already proven it during quiet moments. Maybe he was actually a decent person who cared about her pain and had done his best to soothe it in his own way.

Yet she couldn't be with someone who wasn't honest.

The real Kyle must've noticed her sorrow. She hadn't done a very good job of keeping it in. But she wasn't about to make that mistake again.

"I'm going to get Murphy over here to do some explaining," he said, reaching for his phone.

Tam's temples began banging. A confrontation. Was she ready for this? Or was she just going to lose it in front of Murphy, her carefully constructed barricades dropping like they'd never even existed?

But what else was she going to do? Avoid Murphy forever? All she wanted to do was ask him what had happened. All she wanted was for all these problems to disappear so she could just be with him, plain and simple.

Wait. She had to be stronger than this. She had to keep herself together, because that's all she might have left. Herself.

"How about you talk to him alone when he comes?" Kyle asked, pausing in his dialing and watching her with concern. "You probably have…private things…to talk about."

Grateful for this obvious sacrifice—after all, he'd been betrayed, too—she nodded, reaching out so she could close his phone.

"If you don't mind," she said, "I think I can get him down here in record time. There's a pay phone inside I can use."

She explained that she didn't want Murphy to see Kyle's number on his screen, because she suspected that's what had happened earlier, when he'd shut off her cell and kept it. Most important, she didn't want to give him the opportunity to make up more lies before he arrived here.

Agreeing, Kyle put away his cell, looking as if he'd do anything for her right now. But she didn't want Kyle's pity.

She needed Murphy's answers.

14

MURPHY KNEW THE LOCATION of the café where Tam had asked him to meet her—just down the hill, where strong coffee and pastries attracted a young, hip, upscale crowd.

But he wasn't going for the food. When she'd called—from a pay phone, he assumed, her cell still being in his pocket—there'd been a flatness to her tone. Without her usual enthusiasm, she'd told him that the girls had left and that they could finally talk over some coffee.

At a café. Not alone at the house.

Disturbed by unlikely visions of Kyle somehow having reached her, Murphy had tried to discover why she didn't want to come back home, but she was oddly persistent about having it her way and wouldn't explain anything.

In knots, he arrived at the café to find her sitting with her back to him at a table and staring straight ahead.

Then Kyle stepped out of the doorway.

The breeze groaned around Murphy, the air stale and hard to breathe in. Numb, he glided his hand over Tam's phone in his pocket, as if keeping it hidden would somehow shield her from the impending explosion.

She still hadn't sensed his presence, not until Kyle punished Murphy with a stare so devastating that the poetic justice wasn't lost on him.

Because Murphy had looked at Kyle the same way a little over a week ago, outside the lounge where he'd dumped Tam.

Without a word his cousin nodded at her as if they'd had a long conversation and made plans about what would happen when Murphy arrived. Tam didn't move.

Murphy started to say something to Kyle, but his cousin merely walked away, letting him know with his silence that they'd be talking—or at least Murphy would be—later.

Unbearable. He'd hurt these two people he deeply cared about. He was such a bastard.

Feeling like a dead man walking, Murphy moved in front of Tam, worried about her, wondering if Kyle had comforted her. Wondering if she was so angry at Murphy that she needed revenge more than any kind of comfort.

It took her a moment to meet his gaze. And when she did, it was empty.

Pinpoints of sharpness blinded him, searing into his skull, his chest. His heart thudded, hollow, as if it had been robbed of its rhythm and purpose.

Losing her would strip him of what he'd been looking for all his life, he realized. She was more than just an addiction. He could see that now.

"I'm sorry, Tam."

"Sorry." The word matched her eyes—emotionless.

If Murphy had been hurting before, now it was worse, the pinpoints having turned into blade thrusts that were jamming deeper and deeper into his gut.

"I wanted to tell you earlier," he said, resting his hands on the back of a chair facing her. "I started to, but—"

"I know. Interruptions. So that's what the whole 'I'm not who you think I am' spiel was about?"

He nodded.

"Wow, points for the attempt. But you should've told me the second you walked into the lounge, *don't you think?*"

The final words were like black ice, cold, lethal. Her anguish froze him, making him want to claw for something to keep from crashing.

"You're right," he said. "But I didn't do that."

"Why? What could possibly be a good enough reason for pretending to be another man? *What?*"

Don't tell her about Kyle's rejection, he told himself. *You take the heat. You were the one who wanted to be the daredevil.*

But getting a thrill hadn't been the reason he'd continued, had it? There'd been something more, something that went way beyond just a casual affection for her.

And it'd changed everything.

At the brink of devastation, he couldn't stop himself from laying it all out there: the most basic, heartfelt motivation for his disguise.

"The moment I saw you, Tam, I wanted you. Beyond reason. So badly." His voice cracked on that last word because it didn't nearly cover what he felt for her. "But I had the feeling you wouldn't have any interest in a guy like me. You thought you were going to get Kyle, and he's the kind you seemed to really want."

Her eyes were sheened with tears that she was clearly fighting. "What're you saying?"

Here it was: the moment he was dreading beyond

all others. It was time to expose the drone that he feared he would always be, time to make her fully understand his desire to embrace his new self and leave his stagnation behind.

But she was so disgusted with him already that he couldn't stand the thought of her further rejection. So he met her halfway, unwilling to fully reveal that even though he had a new life, he would always be a little of the old Murphy, too.

But he didn't lie. He made sure of that.

"You were so pumped up for Kyle that I couldn't let you down. And he doesn't intend to be a lawyer, like me, so I didn't want you to see me as the serious type. I wanted you to stay excited about the fancy-free man you were expecting."

It didn't give away too much, but it told her enough.

She was staring at the ground, battling her emotions, and that gave him cause to hang in there.

Yet when she slowly looked up again, the disconnection between them crushed his hopes.

He wanted to shout, *Remember me? You told me things you probably haven't told anyone else, Tam. You trusted me then, and you can do it again. I won't let you down anymore.*

But he couldn't blame her for pushing him away. He of all people knew she'd been rejected enough to earn him a one-way ticket out of her life.

God. Out of her life.

"Could you at least tell me," she said, "who the hell you really are?"

He balked, self-preservation still winning. "I'm Murphy—"

"I know. Murphy Sullivan. Kyle said that."

She wanted to yell at him for working her over, but she understood why he'd done it, all too thoroughly. Hadn't she, in a way, also been pretending to be someone else most of her life through a series of happy faces and costumes? Hadn't she been avoiding her core issues with a pleasant disguise, too?

But she'd never gone as far as Ky—no, *Murphy* had.

Yet there was one thing holding her back from physically ripping into him: how Murphy had wanted to buy her that one drink just to ease the blow of being ditched.

The kind of man who did that was worth a second chance. Wasn't he?

If he hadn't taken that small lie and run with it, yes. But in the end, what was the difference between Murphy and someone like her mom? They'd both constructed calculated "other" lives until they'd been caught.

See, she told herself. No difference at all.

"So who are you?" she demanded, needing to hear this, no matter how much confusion was racking her.

His gray-blue eyes darkened. Who was he? Did *he* know?

When he gestured enquiringly to the chair, she clipped out a nod. But this was no social arrangement, and he seemed to be aware of that.

His eyes locked on her own, his gaze determined. That sent a rogue thrill over her skin.

Ignore it, she thought, *because the attraction is what got you into this trouble.*

"I've been raised, ever since I was a kid, to be a success," he said. "My grades were good, so my parents convinced me to follow in the tradition of a lot of my family and study law."

Visions of long hours and briefcases clouded her mind. And that's exactly why this man had lied, wasn't it? To avoid the sort of impression a so-called free spirit like her would turn away from.

Wary, he seemed to be reading her for such a reaction. But she kept her expression: puzzled anger.

"My parents put me through school without any complaint," he continued, "and I did everything I could to make it easier on the family. I worked odd jobs and aced my classes. They sent me to Tulane to live with relatives because that's where the Sullivans have always gone to law school. I knew that when I started to make a decent salary, I'd pay them back, whether they wanted it or not. At the very least, I'd live up to their expectations. That's what was really important to them, anyway."

Expectations. She recalled him talking about that cousin who worked too much, who put too much pressure on himself. And she'd felt sorry for the poor soul; she'd been thankful that she had Kyle, the wild guy.

Had she been so obvious about this that she'd unwittingly pushed Murphy to keep up his pretenses? If she'd known he was that cousin would she have been turned off and never given him another look? Probably.

Tam stopped herself. She was reaching for a loophole to excuse him. How could there be a future with this man after what he'd done?

But he protected you from knowing Kyle's reason for dumping you.

"Somehow I get the feeling that you don't really want to be a lawyer," she said, voice barely a whisper.

"I came to realize I've been living the wrong life, but…"

His voice trailed off, and Tam thought he didn't need to add anything more. Had she shown him the error of his ways just as emphatically as he'd shown her? Or was that wishful thinking?

He looked as if he was going to say one thing, then seemed to change his mind in favor of something else. "The thing is, I do like the challenges of the work, and I know I'd be a good civil trial lawyer. But, in the end, it's just…"

"Just a job," she finished.

She knew he was recalling what she'd said about her own idealistic search for the right career.

"Your family put a lot into you," she said, trying to keep the edge in her voice. "I'm sure quitting would disappoint them."

He was nodding, cautiously reading her.

The silence said so much. How could it be that they knew certain things about each other so well while at the same time they knew next to nothing?

"But I seem to have already let Kyle down," Murphy said. "I just couldn't stop myself, because I felt more for you than I thought I ever could."

Her heart cracked, allowing another opening, and she knew it showed on her face.

Liar, her defense mechanisms screamed. *He's lied and that won't stop him in the future. Don't allow him to do it anymore.*

"Is that the only reason you did this?" she asked,

wanting to hear him say what Kyle had told her so Murphy could confirm a reason for her to forgive him.

A different kind of determination slashed through his gaze, and he kept his tongue.

Why was he hesitating to tell her about Kyle's rejection? Why wouldn't he want to come off as a hero now that he most needed to?

Unless…

Hope swelled. Unless he cared about the destruction he thought Kyle's rejection would cause. Murphy's charade was deceptive, but something like being dumped for the way you looked could scar a woman forever. He seemed to know that; he'd been protecting her from the knowledge all along.

The truth rattled her: if he cared about her that much, he wouldn't tell her what she was asking him to, even if it meant that he was running the chance of looking like a jerk who'd just been in this game for some fun.

In a way, she wanted him to tell her, thus giving her an excuse to bolt. Yet on the other hand she *wanted* to work this out, even if her instincts were barring her from doing it. She was at war with herself, and one little truth from him would take care of her battle.

"Please be straight with me, Murphy."

Do you care enough not to tell me?

A muscle ticked in his jaw, and she couldn't breathe. She realized that she was playing just as much of a game with him right now as he'd been playing with her, all along.

Jaw tightening, he shook his head, not moving an inch.

Posture stiff, he stood. It killed her to see him keeping strong after being beaten like this.

But…*he cared.*

She couldn't hold back. "I know what Kyle said about me."

He bunched his fists and made a clear attempt to appear as if he didn't understand. "Tam…"

"Kyle thought I was a dog. And you didn't want me to find out, so you came inside to have one drink and make excuses for him, then go on your merry way."

"I never wanted you to know about that."

"But I do," she said, tears rising from her chest, upward. "Don't you know that it doesn't matter now?"

He looked at her as if she was crazy.

"I don't feel unattractive. Not anymore." She cocked her head. "Unless you were just saying all those compliments to butter me up so you could keep getting in my pants."

His gaze was steady. "I meant every word I said about *you,* Tam."

She was split down the middle even though he had passed the loyalty test, but she panicked anyway, because it was so much easier to run away from all this than to stay.

Liar, her dad had said to her mom. *Get out of the house. Don't come back.*

Murphy was repentant now, but what would happen if he found something that was worth covering up in the future?

"I want to forgive you, but…" She pushed at the table in frustration. "I don't want to repeat what I've seen played out over and over again in this world."

He looked as if he was hanging from a ledge and she was the only one who could reach out to him. But she couldn't. There was too much to think about. Too much damage he could still do to her.

"Can you promise me something?" she asked, needing to get out of here, to disappear before she gave in.

"Name it."

His concern dug into her. "I need you to let me go home now, and I need you not to contact me until I've…"

Until what? She couldn't stay with him.

"Don't do this, Tam," he said, rising.

"I have to." She stood, too, desperate to clear her mind of his overwhelming presence, of the memories that were telling her to stay. "I'll be going to a hotel, so don't bother trying to find me." When he made a move to protest, she halted that. "Please. You owe me that much."

Closing his eyes, he managed a nod. Then, reluctantly, he reached into his pocket, brought out her phone. He laid it on the table, as if letting go of it meant letting go of her, too.

She had to leave *now*.

When she reached out to take the cell, her hand brushed his. A furious zing paralyzed her arm, and she all but jumped back, trying to get out of his force field.

"You might not believe it," he said softly, "but every word that made you feel good really was the truth."

Before she could hear more, she took off at a brisk walk, then a run.

Escaping while she could.

THAT NIGHT, as Murphy was about to pick up his phone to call Tam's cell—just to see if she was safe, just to let her know he was going nuts over not knowing where she was—a knock sounded at his apartment door.

When he found Kyle at the threshold, he knew it was time to pay this piper, too.

"If you didn't have such a hangdog look on your face right now, I'd kick your ass," his cousin said. "I don't ever want to hear about what a dick *I* am. After what you did to Tamara—"

"I'm sorry, Kyle."

"You're sorry, all right."

Now Murphy knew exactly what it felt like to be a loser, to be looked down on because he'd screwed up. He also had firsthand knowledge of how someone would look at him differently if that person saw who he really was. And he wasn't just talking about Kyle.

As he'd told Tam about his family and his job, he'd detected a change in the way she'd gazed at him: judging him as a man who was following in the footsteps of her father and mother.

Yup, a workaholic and a liar. He was the best of both worlds.

By this time, Kyle had already sauntered inside and plopped down on a black futon. He leveled the death stare at Murphy. "Man, for a guy who always walks the line, you sure as hell dove over it."

Without much energy, Murphy sank down on a reclining chair across the room. He hunkered over, his forearms on his thighs, heavy with thoughts of what he'd done to Tam. To Kyle.

His near-brother didn't think he was so great now, and he felt the realization shattering his perception of his own identity, his place in the world.

You were destroying that anyway, said that new voice inside of him. *Everything's been torn down in total anarchy. Now's your chance to build it back up again the way you want it to be.*

If you've got the strength.

Meeting Kyle's wounded gaze head-on, Murphy found something to strive for, a place to start rebuilding: the mutual affection they'd had all these years.

Strength, he thought. *It's there.*

"So you did end up getting in touch with her," Murphy said. "And I did everything I could to stop it."

"Can't believe I managed to outsmart you by catching Tamara at home since her cell was *mysteriously* out of order."

Guiltily, Murphy remembered turning off her phone.

"She thought I was you," Kyle continued. "And when I invited her to have coffee, she came."

Murphy wasn't so much interested in the minute details of how that had been accomplished; all he could think about was the devastating outcome.

"An accidental coup," Kyle said, sounding a lot less proud at besting Murphy than he would've expected. There was too much agony there. "You could've just told me what you'd been doing. Why didn't you?"

There was such a plea in the question that Murphy knew no answer would be adequate. Still, he tried.

"Because I knew this would happen." Murphy gestured to Kyle's slumped posture. "The look. It says that I let you down, and I didn't want to face that."

"You gave a crap about what I'd think?"

Murphy could only nod. He didn't trust himself to use his voice.

Eyes brightening, his cousin allowed that to settle. After a moment he said, "You're human, Murph. And

you made a real bad choice. But I still think you're…
well…" Kyle offered a small shrug. "You're still the guy
I'd try to dress like, or be as good as on the basketball
court or in the kitchen or…anything else you excelled
at. Which is everything, by the way."

Chest stinging, Murphy merely nodded again. A
heaviness was lifting from the air—disillusionment
replaced by possible forgiveness.

As they both trudged through this brittle truce, he
caught Kyle glancing at the open cell phone Murphy
had set on the counter that divided his well-stocked
kitchen from where they were sitting.

"She told me not to contact her until she was ready,"
Murphy said, thankful for the reprieve, "then went to
some hotel to cool off. I was thinking of…"

"Calling her?" Kyle seemed just as thankful not to
be getting all emotional about their moment. "Not a
smart move. The worst thing you can do is disrespect
her even more by going against what she wants. I don't
know much, but I do know that you can really whip up
a disaster if you disobey a woman who's already angry."
He plucked at the futon's material. "Tamara's got a lot
to absorb. Kinda like me."

Time to get down to it. "I only meant to have that
one drink.…"

Unbound, the full story spilled out of Murphy: the
relief he'd felt at pretending to be a different person for
just that one night. The belief that another night at the
masquerade would be just as innocuous. The need to
continue for just one *more* night, then another…

"I never planned to feel this way about her, though,"
Murphy finished, throat raw.

For a time Kyle didn't say anything. He looked too thrashed by this change in Murphy to form any words. Instead he kept toying with the futon, as if it were an abacus that was helping him calculate what'd happened.

Finally, he chuffed—a melancholy sound. "And here I thought that a person stopped being surprised by the people he knew by, like, age ten. I guess we never really realize everything about anybody else, huh?"

Murphy thought of how Tam had bared her soul to him during their nights, how he wished things were different so that he could know all her plans, her fears, her hopes.

Because he wanted to. God in heaven, he wanted to know each layer, revel in its intricacies, then return the favor by revealing his own.

His blood started warming at the anticipation of finding her. Dammit, he wanted her back more than anything.

But…Kyle. His cousin needed his attention, too, and Murphy was going to give him the respect he deserved.

"I'm sorry I disappointed you," Murphy said. "I guess it must feel good to know that I'm not this great guy after all."

"It's not like I'm cheering about that." Kyle stopped fidgeting. "Seeing you in trouble like this breaks *my* heart, Murph. It's like—" he cleared his throat, shrugged "—like if you can't get through life unscathed, who can?"

"I've never been perfect, Kyle."

That left a pause.

"Well, you know what they say." Kyle resolutely banged his hand on the seat. "'A man isn't measured by his accomplishments so much as by the way he makes up for his mistakes.'"

Murphy cocked his head. Was Kyle trying to comfort him? "Who said that?"

"Me." He offered a grin. "I made it up. It was fitting."

With a tinge of relief, Murphy and Kyle stared at each other as if really seeing the other for the first time. In recognition, they laughed—cleansing away the conflict.

So much to make up for, Murphy thought. *So much to still do for the people I've failed.*

But, oddly enough, he was going to come out of this a better person. Failure hadn't crushed him as he'd feared. It'd made him even stronger.

He offered a grin to Kyle, and his cousin accepted it by saying, "Can I help with Tamara?"

Spurred by the mention of the woman he needed with every screaming cell in his body, Murphy stood, intending to just dial her up and suffer the consequences.

But then he remembered Kyle's advice and decided his cousin was right. He shouldn't disrespect her wishes, especially after seeming to lack so much respect for her in the first place.

"Have any ideas about how to show her just how sorry I am?" he asked.

"Uh-huh." Kyle looked at Murphy as if his older cousin hadn't learned a damned thing. "How about by just being yourself?"

He flinched at the horror of that. Reveal the ho-hum Murphy who still lingered?

But then the advice sank in, calming him. It was so simple and made so much sense. He didn't have to surprise Tam with a five-star dinner or whisk her off to Paris to tell her how he felt. To expect total forgiveness, he just had to give her the one thing he feared the most: the naked truth.

She would have to accept *all* of him, along with the lies he'd told.

"Just sit down, Murph." Kyle motioned toward the seat. "You ain't going nowhere for a while, so at least make it up to *me* first. It'll be good practice."

At Kyle's cheeky—yet tentatively hopeful—grin, Murphy gladly obliged him by taking a seat.

A new understanding with his cousin was a damned great prize, he told himself.

He only hoped Tam would give him the same chance.

IT WAS LUNCHTIME the next day, and Tam sat on a couch in the bathroom lounge waiting for the Sisters meeting to begin. All day she'd been dragging herself around as if she were wearing weights in the halfhearted, eye-catching Western clothing she'd thrown together for Monday in the office.

Maybe the outfit was an attempt to get back to normal, to reassure herself that she was still a work-in-progress who could deal with pain on her own terms. All the same, the clothes hung on her, drab and artless.

Last night she'd gone home to pack, half hoping Murphy wouldn't pay mind to her request for privacy, half hoping he would. When he hadn't shown—and she couldn't blame him, because he was only doing as she asked—she'd abandoned the hotel plan and decided to stay put, maybe even hoping he would come over.

Which didn't happen, of course.

And even though she suspected Murphy was honorable enough to stay away from her at work, she'd been holding her breath all day, anticipating him crashing through the doors of Dillard Marketing to air their dirty laundry in front of her coworkers. And she'd been ready for it, once again praying both that it wouldn't happen and that it would.

But he'd told her that he wouldn't fly against what she wanted. Deep down, she needed to believe he would stick to his word and give her space. Even though she was aching to see him again.

God, she didn't know what she wanted, did she?

As Pamela strolled into the lounge, she seemed surprised to see Tam and, on both sides of her, Danica and Teena patting Tam's knees in support. They already knew her story and had probably told Pamela, too, but Tam was putting on a happy face and shoving it to the back of her head right now. She wasn't allowing K— *Murphy* to get to her. She was an individual, remember? She could stand on her own.

Despite her bravado, inside she felt the rain of despair drowning her, mirroring the drops that had been falling outside all morning.

Before starting the meeting, Pamela knelt in front of Tam, concern in her eyes. "It's good to see you here."

"I'm fine." Tam widened that smile. She felt as if it was going to break her face apart. "Business as usual."

With a reassuring squeeze to Tam's knee, Pamela smiled back, then got to her feet. Tam barely noticed her friend calling the meeting of the Sisters of the Booty Call to order.

"You're my hero," Danica whispered to Tam as Julia Nguyen volunteered her dating story to start off the festivities.

Her friends knew not to mention what had happened with Kyle/Murphy here. Let everyone assume Tam was okay. Let them look at her façade and think that life was peachy keen and not know any better. That's how Tam wanted it.

Didn't she?

"For now," Julia was saying, cheeks glowing, "I won't be drawing a card. I'm pretty sure I have a real boyfriend!"

Everyone whooped and clapped, even Tam. She was happy for the other woman, who'd been dating the same man for a few weeks. Tam only wished that she was the one making the announcement.

Loneliness spilled through her as Julia described how Gary, her new guy, had taken her to Coit Tower and given her a picnic under the sky.

She barely paid attention to the stories told by the rest of the group in turn. But when Pamela introduced a fresh member—a redheaded banker from downstairs named Jo Ann Green—Tam came to, joining in the welcoming ceremony.

Just like the one she'd gone through not so long ago.

Wistfully she recalled drawing the card from The Boot, never knowing that Kyle would actually be Murphy.

She saw gray-blue eyes looking at her, *into* her, and she longed to be under his gaze again.

Why couldn't she be angry with him? And how could she be, when his motivations had stemmed from just wanting to save her from getting hurt by Kyle's opinion? She could continue to blame him for what had happened, but…jeez, he'd wanted to tell her everything. He'd just been beaten to it when she'd unknowingly sabotaged his confession.

Why did he feel the need to confess? Because he planned to stick around?

Just as hope stretched awake in her, the meeting ended. It'd flown by, and from the looks on her friends' faces, they'd known she hadn't heard more than ten words of it.

But that's why Tam considered them potentially great friends, because as the meeting broke apart, Danica, Teena and Pamela hugged her wordlessly, then Danica linked her arm through Tam's and escorted her back to the office. It was as if they knew what she needed.

Just as Murphy had.

Back at her cubicle, she entered numbers until her mind cleared. The symbols were meaningless, chaff flying by her vision as her mind clogged with thoughts about Murphy Sullivan.

Later, when she went home, the rain was just beginning to settle into a melancholy patter. She barely felt it as she walked from the bus stop without an umbrella, water sprinkling on her head and clothes.

She stepped onto the porch and unlocked the door. When she opened it, the ghosts of Murphy, the man she thought she'd known, wrapped her in the memories of their lovemaking, their afterglows.

Drained, Tam leaned against the doorjamb, wanting to go in, but too anguished to do so. She'd been hoping he would be waiting here for her, even against her wishes.

But he hadn't come back. Maybe he hadn't cared enough to.

And that's when, at her lowest point, a voice sounded from behind her.

15

THE SECOND MURPHY had seen her, his body had thundered within, a quiet storm like the one trickling here outside. He'd been waiting in a dark corner of the porch, yearning to be with her.

"The past twenty-four hours have been hell without you," he said softly.

She spun around, hand to her throat, beautiful turquoise eyes wide. His quirky Tam, dressed in cowboy boots, a long prairie skirt and blouse, and a fringed vest, all damp with rain. Water had curled her hair and beaded on her skin.

He ran a hungry gaze over her; if it'd been his hands, they would've torn off her clothing.

Her chest rose up and down, marking the passing seconds with taut silence. Something was stirring in her eyes, and it wasn't just passion. It was an emotion he'd begun to feel, also. Keenly.

Murphy urged himself on, confident enough not to revert to the polite bookworm and bow out. Not anymore.

"I didn't get much sleep last night," he said. "Kyle came over, and then after he left, I sat there staring at the phone, wondering how angry you'd be if I called you." Murphy took a purposeful step forward. "But I decided to lay off, like you asked me to, even if it kept me awake and made me next to useless at the firm today. Then—" he lifted his hands, wanting so badly to just touch her "—then I came here because I couldn't stay away. Not for another minute."

Her fingers were still at her throat, but they had relaxed, as if his words were slowly persuading her. But it was still a sign of defensiveness, a reminder of everything that had come between them.

The rain stuttered on the awning, rolling down to the bushes and grass.

After the longest pause Murphy had ever endured, Tam bit her lip, then finally held the door open, silently inviting him in. She turned her back on him and headed away, but Murphy's pulse quickened in spite of that.

He was back inside. The first step to winning her over.

He tracked her to the kitchen, where she was standing by the door and using a hand towel to dry her hair. Through the window, the backyard foliage shimmered with rain.

She stopped suddenly, as if aware of what was now consuming him, too: the memory of the night he'd dried the rain out of her hair, off her body.

Longing rushed him like a flash flood. "Tam."

She stared at the towel. It was trembling in her hands.

Just be yourself, Kyle had said.

Without stopping to analyze, he went with his instincts and laid himself bare for her, no matter what the cost.

"I'm not just a guy who was working to be a lawyer," he said. "That's only the surface. I'll admit, I have been boring, stale, unwilling to take a step out of my comfort zone." He made a fist, then spread it apart. "I've been a cog in a machine. And there're still parts of me that haven't changed—they never will, I suspect. That's just the person I am, and that's why I wanted to be with you. I needed to see how far I could push myself and to forget about everything for a night, then two, then three.... And I thought that if you believed I was actually capable of doing that, you'd want me, too."

She didn't respond, so he took a deep breath, then went for it.

"But *all* of me, Tam, fell for you." His heartbeat heated his ears, filled them with pounding drums. "I fell in love with you."

Outside, the rain tapped, rustling the trees.

Tam's hair was hanging over her face, obscuring her reaction.

Rejection, he thought, feeling as if darkness was swallowing him. *Here it comes, even though you tried to cheat it, Murphy.*

The rain kept falling, each drop seeming like an hour.

Then, quietly, her voice filtered through her wet curls. "But how can this be love?"

Like a survivor who'd taken cover from an explosion, his heart stirred, opening up slowly to assess the damage. She hadn't yet thrown him out because he was so wrong for her. No, she was testing.

Could she actually begin to accept everything about him?

"I mean…" Tam parted her hair to reveal eyes shiny with tears. "I can barely even remember to call you by your real name."

Tears, Murphy thought. Sadness? Or was there a gleam of hope there, too?

Pressing on, he said, "Somewhere along the way, the unexpected happened, didn't it? You revealed things to me that I doubt you've ever shared with anyone else, and I saw something in you that I've never seen in anyone before. And I think you—"

"Stop, Murphy."

"—started feeling something for me, too."

There it was.

Adrenaline pumped through him again, vibrating like stretched wire in the wind. Yet this time it wasn't a matter of seeing how much he could get away with.

He was offering her what he'd never dreamed of giving anyone. His love.

Would she throw it back in his face?

From the way she was clutching the towel, he wasn't sure.

Go, Murphy. Don't let her get away.

Cautiously, confidently, he went to her, took the towel from her hands and cupped her face, forcing her to look him in the eyes.

"Tell me that you don't feel anything for me," he said. "And I'll leave. I'll never bother you again."

"I can't."

"Then tell me what you do feel, Tam. Just *tell* me."

A tear emerged from one eye, rushing down her face as if it were embarrassed to be seen and needed to hide. "I'm afraid."

"Of what?"

"Of…"

He could pretty much guess the answer. Her parents' divorce had broken something inside of her. But Murphy could repair it—he *knew* he could.

"I'll try my hardest never to let you down again." He stroked the tear's trail, erasing the dampness. "It's a big step, Tam, but if you believe in me, I'll earn back your trust. I'll give you every reason to risk being with me."

"I…" Another teardrop fell, and she buried the side of her face against one of his hands. "I want to. But this is hard. Aside from the trust issues and this entire trial, it's hard because…"

Oh, God, here it came. *We're not right for each other.* His worst nightmare realized.

She looked up at him with those vivid blue eyes filled with pain.

"For all these years," she said, "I've had such a thick skin. It got that way from telling myself every day that nothing could hurt me—not my mom or the guys who always disappointed me. It was easier to just act like a happy girl who's into her clothing or decorating. That way, people don't ask questions about what's wrong. They look at everything I've created around me and not any further. I was an individual, all right—standing alone."

"Individuality isn't about what you wear," he said, needing to comfort her. "It's about accepting what you've got on the inside and feeling good about it."

By now, more tears were wetting her cheeks. "Pushing people into the wrong impression of who I was…that was comfortable for me. But then you came along."

"And what?" She couldn't avoid *this.* He wouldn't let her. "What, Tam?"

"And…" She closed her eyes, smiling and crying at the same time. "I went and fell for you, too, because I need someone who understands me. The Kyle you

thought you were never could've done that. I like his—
your—lightheartedness, but there's so much more to
love than that." She hitched in a sob. "At least, I think
it's love that I feel for you. I wouldn't know. I'm *terri-
fied* to know."

Murphy's heart seemed to rule his body, a warm,
beating mass that made him feel ten times more alive
than ever. Even in the face of his fears, she was accepting him, heart and soul.

Overcome, he scooped her into his arms, kissed her
and savored the taste of her tears. He and Tam had a
long way to go with each other, but this was a start. A
new life, for both of them.

He tangled his fingers in her hair as he worked his
mouth over hers, hot and wet, giving and taking at the
same time.

Running a finger down her face to collect a tear, he
disengaged, then kissed her softly again.

"It's got to be love," he said against her mouth. "You'd
never come this close to forgiving me if it wasn't."

Her hands were fervently roaming over his back, as
if refamiliarizing themselves with his shape. Under her
caresses, Murphy's flesh blazed with fire, as if every
touch were a brand with her name on it.

"I missed you," she said. "This was the longest day
of my life. When I left yesterday, I felt like I'd
lost…well, my best friend. And I was so angry that you
could make me feel that way."

He was stroking her neck, her jawline, so damned
happy to be allowed the privilege again. At his touch,
she seemed to change right before his eyes; it was a
repeat of that first time, when he'd seen her sitting at

that table in the lounge, sad and lacking confidence, and then she'd smiled, making him smile back, and she'd glowed for the next week.

Had she come around? Truly?

"Things are so muddled," she said, "that I'm not sure where we go from here."

"I go back to being honest, for a start."

"Kyle vouched for you up and down. So I know that this is the first time you've ever messed up."

He would've liked to have said it was the last, but he knew part of changing himself had to do with facing and accepting flaws.

Not that he was going to *try* to mess up again.

"I just need to figure out how to be Murphy and Kyle at the same time without hurting anyone," he said.

"That can't be too hard." Tam rested her mouth against the backs of his hands, as if slowly absorbing him. "First, I suppose you do what your instincts have been telling you to do—as long as it doesn't affect other people in a bad way."

Panic should've shaken him. It didn't. In particular, he thought about Ian's firm, and knew that he wasn't going to be sticking around. He'd turned it over in his mind so often lately that it wasn't a shock to his system anymore.

She tentatively fitted herself against him, as if to reassure herself that they were still a match.

As they fused—yeah, a perfect fit, all right—her smile returned full force.

"We'll make it through all the changes," he said. "I have no doubt about that, because not being with you isn't an option."

She closed her eyes, one more tear leaking past her

lashes. Then, slowly she opened her gaze, a blue as clear as a lake you take for granted when you pass by it every day until you stop to appreciate its beauty.

"Then let's see if we can enjoy ourselves again," she said finally, leading him outside. "Let's see if we still work."

Before he answered, she started walking backward and tilting her face to the wet sky, just as she had a few nights ago.

Back then, he'd missed his chance to play in the rain, to fully become the man he was yearning to be. To be her partner in so many ways.

But he wasn't going to let the opportunity go by this time.

No. Instead he followed her into the shower, laughing, his mouth parted to take in the fresh elixir. It glided down his throat, settled in his belly and made him more complete than ever.

From a few feet away, Tam smiled, the rain washing away the tracks of tears from her face.

He smiled, too, falling in love all over again.

TAM'S CHEST WAS NEAR to bursting as she watched the rain soaking Murphy's hair and his white button-down shirt.

The thin material sucked to his muscles, becoming a piece of clothing with new significance. It wasn't drab corporate wear now. It was a sexy hint of the skin beneath it, an invitation to join him in soul *and* body. She began to ache, not just between her legs, but all over.

Under his persuasion, she'd dashed away her greatest terrors and admitted it: she loved him.

Loved him.

Scary, exciting…it was a concoction of the two. But all she knew was that she had more burgeoning hope than ever, and Murphy had given that to her.

There was a possibility that they could do anything together, she thought, anything at all if they tried hard enough.

Impetuously she unbuttoned her vest, shucked it off and tossed it to the covered kitchen steps. She did the same with her boots and stockings, then twirled around, feeling truly free for the first time in her life.

Because she'd admitted to what had been growing in her heart.

Murphy laughed, too, taking off his shoes and socks to feel the grass under his feet, just like her. He darted over to scoop her in his arms and whirl her around until her legs spun out. Two kids, playing in the rain without a care in the world.

When he caught her up in a kiss, the rain made it slick.

A bolt of liquid electricity shot through her, and she threw caution aside now, responding with all the passion she'd stored up through the years because she was trusting him to keep it safe. She gnawed at him, hungry, their tongues sliding past each other's lips, stroking, seeking. Slow, deep thrusts, carnal and drenched with urgency.

The rain made their clothing heavy, and she fumbled with his shirt buttons, tugged the material from his torso and let it fall to the grass. The risk of being seen by someone only aroused her more.

"I want to hear you say my real name, Tam," he growled in her ear. "But I want you to *feel* it."

There he was—the bad boy.

Murphy, she thought. It was the real man, not an act. He'd risked a lot in coming to her today, revealing everything. Accepting him was her own proof of courage.

He yanked off her saturated blouse, her skirt, leaving her in bra and undies. Skillfully, he undid the bra, gently but insistently pulling her arms upward as he bound her wrists with the lace. He rubbed his chest against hers, skin on skin, wet friction against her sensitive nipples.

Explosive. Oh, she wanted to burst apart.

She could feel his erection building against her as he brushed her crotch and kept her arms raised.

Breathing hard, they both looked into each other's eyes as the rain beat down. Droplets ran over his face, into his mouth. Turned on, she surged forward, licked his lips, then guided him into another starved kiss.

Soon he slid his mouth down her chin, to her ear, lips tickling her lobe as he spoke. "My name," he said, "I want you to scream it."

"When it's time," she said, voice strained.

"Tease."

But she knew he was getting off on that.

He eased his hands along her arms, still stretched above her, bound by lace, by his wishes. It was a combination she liked—being controlled and not being controlled.

Water sluiced over her skin, and his fingers followed the path of the rain, thumbs tracing down into the curves of her underarms and tickling.

She bucked against him, nudging his hardness.

"Just that much closer to making you scream," he said.

Lower, lower. His palms covered her breasts,

kneading them, encouraging her to move her hips against him.

Her grinding made Murphy's penis pound with all the blood rushing to it, stiffening it. His cock palpitated against his pants, pushing against the material, into the rain-soaked, lace-covered cleft of her.

He wanted to take her now, but he waited. Making her happy was the most important thing. It was a way of showing her she could trust him, that he wouldn't give in to selfish desire and satisfy himself before he could do his best for her.

Instead, he breathed deeply, allowing the moment to unfurl.

With deliberation, he ran his mouth from her throat down to the center of her chest, where he tongue-kissed the skin between her breasts. The taste of rain—clean and pure—spiked through him, mingling with the musk of her flesh to make him drunk.

As he laved a nipple, he coaxed a hand down over her belly, over the firm, warm flatness of it, and slipped into her panties. He combed through her pubic hair, parted the slicked, thickened wetness of her sex and delved inside with two fingers.

She caught her breath and grabbed on to him, digging her nails into his back with her still-bound hands. He grunted, gave her nipple an extra emphatic suck, but didn't stop.

Nail marks. He'd take that punishment.

In, out…his fingers were coated with her juices, his thumb working her clit and making her gyrate while his mouth pulled at her breast.

"Murphy…"

His name.

A snap of raging desire rocked him at the thought of what had risen from the ashes of his charade.

Completeness, he thought.

Tam.

As she started to cry out, Murphy lowered them to the soaked grass, knowing she was ready for him.

They'd happened to settle on a patch of dirt near an herb garden, and mud squished under his knees and shins as he stripped Tam's panties from her.

"Come on," she said, as he rid himself of his pants. "Come on, Murphy."

"That's not a scream."

Roughly he secured a condom from his wallet, freed it and rolled it over his penis. Then, hovering over her, he took the time to absorb her with one long look.

Her arms were over her head, the bra hanging from her wrists. Her hair was spread over the grass, her body coated with streaks of mud like sensuous tattoos, ones that were disappearing with the soft, continuing raindrops.

Reaching up for him, she seemed to take in what he wasn't saying out loud. That his cousin Kyle had been so wrong in his initial impression of her. That her beauty was more complicated and powerful than a first glance could hold.

In one fluid move, he hooked her leg over his upper arm, spreading her open for him. The brown hair between her legs framed the plump red of glistening sex, and his penis jerked in readiness.

Unable to stand it anymore, he drove into her, and she cried out.

But it wasn't the scream he wanted.

Circling his hips, he pushed her from whimpers to an escalating moan. As the mud sloshed around them, he lifted her leg higher, allowing him to go deeper. She anchored her other leg behind one of his, but the mud wouldn't allow them to gain purchase.

They slipped and slid, her voice building as the rain tapped his back, her nails abrading his skin as she grabbed onto him. Something snarled in his chest, trying to get all the way out, while she churned against him.

"Mur…Murph…" she groaned.

The snarl grew into an aggressive growl, his cock on the edge of bursting.

He pushed harder, thrusting, hammering—

"Murph…" She cried out, one time, two times.

Buffeting, pummeling…

The growl turned into a roar that constricted his body.

"Ah…" She stiffened, arched against him. *"Murphy!"*

He spun into a beast flying through the air, screeching and flying until it landed on its prey. With the crash of contact, Murphy seemed to scatter apart.

Beneath him Tam grasped at his shoulders, heaving out great breaths of ecstasy.

As he lost strength and collapsed, holding her against him, the heat of her skin pulled him back together, melding them into each other.

"Murphy," she sighed contentedly against his throat.

It wasn't another scream, but it meant so much more.

A smile took him over as he kissed her.

As the rain washed them bare and free.

Epilogue

A WEEK LATER, Tam and Murphy traveled to nearby Novato, where they looked at a vacant space for rent— a space that, someday, might make both their ambitions come true.

"Wouldn't this be something?" she asked as Murphy walked over the hardwood floor.

It had two stories and reminded Tam of what a bordello might've looked like way back when. She could see the colors—maroon and gold—flaring through the room. Could imagine the polished wood of a staircase, the linen tablecloths in the loft and the gilded touches that would make it striking.

"This is it," Murphy said, sticking his hands in his jeans pockets and grinning that killer grin at her.

Her knees went weak at his smile. They were talking about moving into his Sunset District apartment together; things were serious enough to even encourage a visit from her dad.

After the third-degree—during which at no time had they talked about Murphy's stint as "Kyle"—her dad had approved of Tam's choice in men. In fact, he hadn't even chided her for wanting to move out of his beloved house. Surprisingly, his visit had also given her the guts to broach the subject of his misplaced affections. Houses instead of people. Gathering material things he could hold on to instead of facing his failed marriage. Now, thank goodness, they were hoping to work on healing, just as much as she and Murphy had been working toward it.

"Do you think investors will go for this?" Tam asked.

"Why wouldn't they?"

"I don't know, maybe because we're novices?"

"Oh, hell." He looked happy. So happy and relaxed. "A family-style New-Orleans-type joint. That's something you can't find everyday around here."

They'd planned everything: during his search for capital, he would still tend bar so he could pay off his debts. And he was easing out of his job at Ian's firm because of his decision not to practice law.

But Ian was cool with that. In fact, he'd already told them that he wanted to put money into this venture—a business that they hoped would get Murphy in the clear financially. Murphy's parents hadn't been as easy to assuage, though—they'd been devastated at their son's choice. Still, he was determined to persuade them to come around to the reality: this was what he wanted to do, and he would always be a loving part of their family no matter what his career was.

Especially since Murphy wasn't going to be the only Sullivan involved in this restaurant.

Kyle strolled out from the other walled-off room. "I can picture it, can't you?" He smiled at Tam. "With the way this place'll look, it won't just be the food that brings 'em."

She reveled under his compliment. They liked her decorating ideas, and once the restaurant got started, she was going to help run it. Yup, this was just one of many projects she was definitely going to finish.

But they'd vowed to each other that they would never become workaholics. Murphy had been the first to bring that up.

She trusted that he wouldn't, too. One hundred percent.

As if sensing her thoughts, Murphy came to stand next to her, gathered her in his arms and changed that to a hundred and ten.

Her risk taker, she thought. My God, they were really going to do this.

From across the room, Kyle watched them, his smile growing wistful. With his gung-ho attitude about developing a business, Bridget and Gerald had seen what he could be capable of. And in spite of their disappointment in Murphy, they were happy with Kyle, even though they'd always loved him before.

"Why so blue?" Tam asked.

"Nothing."

But Tam knew. After Murphy's success, he'd been vocal about wanting to find a woman who, as Kyle put it, "Makes me as drunk as my cousin." And she would do anything to help him.

"You're going to have a business card soon, right?" she asked, remembering how Kyle's name had been written on Julia Nguyen's card because he'd been lacking one.

He seemed to know where she was going with this. "As soon as I have a restaurant."

"When you do, give it to me."

At his pleased nod, Tam knew she could recommend him to the Sisters. Because she was still working at Dillard until the restaurant materialized, she visited the meetings on an honorary basis. All the women said that she—along with Julia Nguyen, who'd already gotten engaged with stunning speed—gave them hope.

"Thanks, Tam," Kyle said.

"Yeah, thanks, Tam." Murphy gave her *that* look, the one that said he loved everything about her.

Catching on, Kyle excused himself, knowing when to leave Tam and Murphy alone.

"Just another reason to love you, I suppose," he said, playing with the curly, wild hair that she'd grown to appreciate mostly because Murphy had done so first. "Look at you, helping out my poor cousin."

"Oh, don't get me mushy and reciting all the reasons to love *you*."

Her smile glowed—she didn't need a mirror to know because it was reflected on his face. He seemed to melt at the sight of it.

"Wow." He framed her jaw in his hands. "How can it still surprise me when you knock me over, Tam?"

"Me?" She motioned to her vintage jeans and T-shirt. Shabby chic, but nothing distracting. She'd decided that she would dress up every once in a while, but only when she felt like it. There was no longer a need for defensive wardrobe distractions, because Murphy didn't require them.

"Yeah, you," he said, growing serious now. "Only you."

And as Tam reached up to draw him to her, she knew that he'd see through those distractions, anyway.

Just as she'd ended up seeing right into the heart of him.

Hidden in the secrets of antiquity, lies the unimagined truth...

Introducing

a brand-new line filled with mystery and suspense, action and adventure, and a fascinating look into history.

And it all begins with DESTINY.

In a sealed crypt in France, where the terrifying legend of the beast of Gevaudan begins to unravel, Annja Creed discovers a stunning artifact that will seal her destiny.

Available every other month starting July 2006, wherever you buy books.

GOLD EAGLE®

GRA1

Stability is highly overrated....

Dana Logan's world had always revolved around her children. Now they're all grown up and don't seem to need anything she's able to give them. Struggling to find her new identity, Dana realizes that it's about time for her to get "off her rocker" and begin a new life!

Off Her Rocker

by Jennifer Archer

Page-turning drama...

Exotic, glamorous locations...

Intense emotion and passionate seduction...

Sheikhs, princes and billionaire tycoons...

This summer, may we suggest:

THE SHEIKH'S DISOBEDIENT BRIDE
by Jane Porter

On sale June.

AT THE GREEK TYCOON'S BIDDING
by Cathy Williams

On sale July.

THE ITALIAN MILLIONAIRE'S VIRGIN WIFE

On sale August.

With new titles to choose from every month,
discover a world of romance in our books written
by internationally bestselling authors.

It's the ultimate in quality romance!

Available wherever Harlequin books are sold.

www.eHarlequin.com

HPGEN06

If you enjoyed what you just read,
then we've got an offer you can't resist!

Take 2 bestselling love stories FREE!

Plus get a FREE surprise gift!

Clip this page and mail it to Harlequin Reader Service®

IN U.S.A.	**IN CANADA**
3010 Walden Ave.	P.O. Box 609
P.O. Box 1867	Fort Erie, Ontario
Buffalo, N.Y. 14240-1867	L2A 5X3

YES! Please send me 2 free Harlequin® Blaze™ novels and my free surprise gift. After receiving them, if I don't wish to receive anymore, I can return the shipping statement marked cancel. If I don't cancel, I will receive 6 brand-new novels each month, before they're available in stores! In the U.S.A., bill me at the bargain price of $3.99 plus 25¢ shipping and handling per book and applicable sales tax, if any*. In Canada, bill me at the bargain price of $4.47 plus 25¢ shipping and handling per book and applicable taxes**. That's the complete price and a savings of at least 10% off the cover prices—what a great deal! I understand that accepting the 2 free books and gift places me under no obligation ever to buy any books. I can always return a shipment and cancel at any time. Even if I never buy another book from Harlequin, the 2 free books and gift are mine to keep forever.

151 HDN D7ZZ
351 HDN D72D

Name	(PLEASE PRINT)	
Address	Apt.#	
City	State/Prov.	Zip/Postal Code

Not valid to current Harlequin® Blaze™ subscribers.

Want to try two free books from another series?
Call 1-800-873-8635 or visit www.morefreebooks.com.

* Terms and prices subject to change without notice. Sales tax applicable in N.Y.
** Canadian residents will be charged applicable provincial taxes and GST.
   All orders subject to approval. Offer limited to one per household.
   ® and ™ are registered trademarks owned and used by the trademark owner and/or its licensee.

BLZ05   ©2005 Harlequin Enterprises Limited.

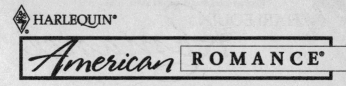

HARLEQUIN *Romance*

A family saga begins to unravel
when the doors to the Bella Lucia
Restaurant Empire are opened...

The Brides of Bella Lucia

*A family torn apart by secrets,
reunited by marriage*

AUGUST 2006

Meet Rachel Valentine, in
HAVING THE FRENCHMAN'S BABY
by Rebecca Winters

Find out what happens when a night of passion is followed
by a shocking revelation and an unexpected pregnancy!

SEPTEMBER 2006

The Valentine family saga continues with
THE REBEL PRINCE by Raye Morgan